Love

NEVER FAILS

NEVER FAILS

J. C. LAFLER

REDEMPTION
PRESS

Published by Redemption Press, PO Box 427, Enumclaw, WA 98022.

Toll-Free (844) 2REDEEM (273-3336)

Redemption Press is honored to present this title in partnership with the author. The views expressed or implied in this work are those of the author. Redemption Press provides our imprint seal representing design excellence, creative content, and high quality production.

Scripture taken from the New King James Version®. Copyright © 1982 by Thomas Nelson. Used by permission. All rights reserved.

ISBN 13: 978-1-64645-350-4 (Paperback)
978-1-64645-343-6 (Hard Cover)
978-1-64645-341-2 (ePub)
978-1-64645-342-9 (Mobi)

Library of Congress Catalog Card Number: 2021900229

Dedication

While the characters in my books are always fictional, a lot of them are based on my own experiences and relationships.

I have a very dear aunt and uncle who have encouraged me without fail throughout my life. I would like to dedicate this novel to my Uncle Darrell and Aunt Marcia Vanvleet, who continue to support and encourage me to this day. Their belief in my abilities, and the love and positivity they have expressed throughout my life, mean more than they will ever know. Thank you from the bottom of my heart.

I would also like to express appreciation to all of the dog lovers out there. Our own little Maltipoo, Bella Rose, looks much like the puppy in this novel. She is a constant source of love and companionship. I hope all of you who have fur babies experience this source of unconditional love.

Watch, stand fast in the faith,
be brave, be strong.
Let all that you do be done with love.

1 Corinthians 16:13–14

NKJV

Prologue

OLIVIA ROBERTS DROVE ALONG the quiet Texas road with her eight-year-old daughter, Bella, chatting happily behind her in the back seat. Oh, to be young and innocent and so happy about getting to go to a birthday party. Bruce hadn't wanted her to go, but for once Olivia had trumped him. And he was furious. Olivia knew she was going to hear more about it when she got back.

"You spoil that kid rotten!" Bruce had yelled. "We don't have money for that crap."

"I can pick something up at the dollar store for next to nothing. Kids her age like everything. Let her be a kid for once."

"She has chores, and she needs to earn her keep. Besides, we need every penny you make to pay the bills. You aren't cutting your shift to take her, are you?"

"Of course not. I don't work this Saturday. I'm working sixty hours this week. They won't let me work more than that. I'll see you tonight."

That had been two days ago, and Olivia had worked long shifts ever since. Looking in the rearview mirror at her happy little girl, she was glad she had stuck to her guns. She had worked ten p.m. to ten a.m. and come straight to her brother's house to pick up her daughter and take her to the party. Knowing she had a twelve-hour shift, Olivia had arranged for Bella to spend the night with Paul and his wife, Eleanor. They loved having Bella, since they didn't have kids of their own, and had picked her up after school on Friday. Paul and Eleanor were happy to take her to get something for her little friend. Bruce didn't need to know that. It was really none of his business.

She had met Bruce a little over six months ago, when she had taken her car to have the brakes checked out. The local auto repair shop near the hospital was a logical choice, and Bruce was working there. He had shown interest in her and talked her into having lunch after the repairs were made. Olivia had few friends and most of her free time was reserved for her daughter, so spending time with Bruce had seemed special. When he talked to her about sharing an apartment to save money a few weeks later, she thought it sounded like a good idea. She was struggling to make ends meet herself, and the extra income would be a blessing. It wasn't long before she realized it was a huge mistake.

Bruce hadn't contributed a dime so far, claiming he lost his job the day after they moved in. He had plenty of time to fret about every move they made, but never found time to look for another job. She couldn't carry the financial load forever. And he ate all the groceries she bought, even Bella's special treats.

It hadn't taken Olivia long to figure out that Bruce was happy to live off what she made. And she was afraid he hated her daughter, because he found fault with everything she did and never had a kind word to say to her. He was critical of how she did her chores and often made her redo them while he watched and heckled her. Olivia couldn't tolerate it and really needed to find a way to get him out of their life for good. But it was going to be difficult. She had discovered he had a horrible temper, and at times he scared her to death! Her brother had warned her about moving in with someone like Bruce. Paul was more than ten years her senior, and he was all she had left, but she had still pushed his advice aside.

Distracted by her own thoughts, Olivia didn't see the old truck coming up fast behind her until it was too late. It bumped hard into the rear of her car and veered off, trying to come up alongside her on the passenger side where her daughter was sitting and screaming in fear. Seeing that the truck was planning to crash into her car on that side, she raced ahead of it and whipped the steering wheel with all her might to the left and slammed on the brakes. Her car screeched to a halt. Now the driver came directly at *her*!

Bella screamed.

The truck crashed into them like a wrecking ball.

Unbearable pain exploded in her head.

Chapter 1

BELLA UNLOCKED THE DOOR of the quaint, cottage-style house she had shared for over two decades with her aunt and uncle. It was still hard to believe they were both gone. She smiled, picturing her uncle's tall, slightly bent frame that was such a contrast to his petite wife.

Aunt Eleanor had passed during Bella's second year of student teaching, and now her precious Uncle Paul was gone too. Pushing her straight, light-brown hair behind her ears, she eased her heavy backpack off her shoulders. Rubbing them to release the tension, she wished she could remove the heaviness from her heart as easily.

Almost a year now, but Bella could still picture her uncle sitting at the table working on his latest puzzle. So sad to think they would never work on another one, laughing and talking about anything and everything while they fit the tiny pieces together. Though Bella was petite like her aunt, she had inherited her uncle's love of puzzles and reading. Over the years, Aunt Eleanor had often commented that they were like two peas in pod. They were always happy sharing the same space, enjoyed similar activities and loved being silly together. She often accused them of keeping her from getting her work done, but they pulled her right into their love and laughter anyway. If only they were both still here with her. But then Bella knew from experience that good things didn't last forever.

She carried her purse into the bedroom that was hers now. She had bought a new mattress for the double bed after her uncle passed and moved into the room that reminded her every day of the unconditional love her aunt and uncle had lavished on her. She had become the child they could never have, and they had called her their gift from God. She had used the twin bed in the spare room over the years, but the double bed was where her aunt had held her and comforted her many times, starting with the night Bruce dropped her off at this very house. She was only eight when it happened, still grieving for her mom who had been killed just days before. She was tired and sore from the accident, but she could remember that day in great detail. She would never forget the words Bruce had hurled at her.

"You killed her, you know. It's your fault," he had screamed at her. "You had to go to that stupid birthday party."

She still felt guilty after all this time, the weight of it compounded by years of feeling the loss of her mother. Even the love that had been lavished on her hadn't been able to take it away. But at least *he* was out of her life. Bruce had taken everything they had and disappeared. *Good riddance.* Bella's thoughts mimicked the words her uncle had said more than once.

Shaking off memories she really didn't want to recall, she left the bedroom. Bella tried not to let the sadness overwhelm her as she put the kettle on for some tea. She shivered, even though it was still warm outside, remembering that Aunt Eleanor always said, "Tea makes everything better."

Thinking of her aunt brought her uncle to mind almost immediately. She could remember him standing right where she stood today.

"And now abide faith, hope, love, these three," Uncle Paul would say. Uncle Paul had been an elder at their church, and they had created a little game over the years of her uncle reciting part of a verse from the Bible and expecting Bella to reply with the rest of the verse and name the book of the Bible it came from. The number of verses he knew had always astonished her. Without thinking about what she was doing, she spoke out loud.

"But the greatest of these is love. 1 Corinthians 13:13. I love and miss you so much, Uncle."

Chapter 2

THE NEXT MORNING, BELLA headed to her teaching job at the school feeling better and glad that it was Friday. She was looking forward to a quiet weekend, a little shopping on Saturday with her best friend, and church on Sunday. Church always revived her and made her feel close to her aunt and uncle.

"Good morning, Miss Roberts," most of the students said in unison as she entered the classroom and raised her hand, her signal for them to quiet down.

"Good morning, students. I hope you all studied your spelling words."

Friday mornings were spelling contests, and Bella gave everyone a chance to join in. She was pleased when one of her students, Tess Jones, agreed to participate. Tess was a great student academically but very shy. Bella sensed it probably had something to do with the fact that her clothing was generally too small and not very clean. She tried hard to encourage Tess, knowing from her own experience that having clean clothes that fit wasn't always easy.

After almost twenty minutes, Bella was happy to see that Tess was one of two students still standing. The other student was Gabe Smith, an exceptionally bright young man who tended to be overconfident and had a bit of a temper.

"Your turn, Gabe. The next word is stupidity."

Without hesitation he started to spell. "S-t-u-p-i-d-i-d-y, stupididy." Looking around the classroom, he beamed, sure that he had it right.

"I'm sorry, Gabe, that is incorrect. Tess, please spell the word stupidity."

"S-t-u-p-i-d-i-t-y, stupidity." Bella heard the nervous quaver as Tess spelled the word.

"That is correct, Tess. You are the champion speller this week." Bella retrieved the little trophy from her desk that signified the winner. The student who won on Friday got to display the trophy on their desk until a new winner was announced at the next spelling contest. Before she could give it to Tess, Gabe had stormed to the front of the room.

"I spelled it right too," he complained loudly. "You must have heard me wrong. You have to give us another word."

"I'm sorry, Gabe," Bella explained. "You used a *d* instead of a *t*."

"No, no I didn't! You didn't listen. I spelled it right. I know I did."

Glancing around the room at the surprised looks and whispers, Bella knew the class was waiting to see what she would do. "I'm sorry, Gabe, but you used the wrong letter. I heard it very clearly. Please take your seat. You can try again next week." She tried not to notice Gabe as he stomped back to his seat, glaring at her.

"Congratulations, Tess. Great job studying the spelling words this week." She handed Tess the trophy and waited for her to return to her seat.

The rest of the morning went by without incident, and it was lunchtime before Bella knew it. She took her lunch to the teachers' lounge, making a list of a few things she wanted to pick up the next day. Once she finished eating, she tucked the list in her pocket and made her way back to her room.

Bella's classroom was noisy when she entered, but a hush fell over it as soon as the students noticed her. Tess was crying, holding the trophy that was now in pieces.

"Can someone tell me what happened, please?" Bella walked over to Tess, handed her a tissue, and took the broken trophy.

Caroline, the student most likely to spill the beans, didn't fail to provide an answer. "Gabe broke it on purpose because he didn't win. And he called Tessa bad names too. He told her she cheated, and he would make sure she couldn't display it on her desk. Then he put it on the floor and stomped on it. He told us if we told what happened, we'd be sorry. But I'm not afraid of him. He's just being a bully, and that's against the law." Caroline glared at Gabe across the room.

"Gabe, could I see you out in the hall, please?" Bella followed as he all but ran out of the room amid comments from the class. She heard "I told you so" and "You're in trouble" while she closed the door behind them.

"Would you like to tell me what happened?" she asked quietly.

"It's just like Caroline told you." Gabe wouldn't look at her at all, just stared at his very expensive-looking, shiny black shoes. What fourth grader wore shoes like that?

"You know I am going to have to call your parents, Gabe. I'm extremely disappointed in you. You've won that trophy before, and you were so proud of it. And you will have the opportunity to win it again. Why would you be so mean? Tess earned the championship today, and it was wrong to blame her for your mistake. You know that, right?"

"I'm sorry, I'm sorry," Gabe replied quickly. Bella could see a look of pure panic on his face, and was that fear as well? She actually felt sorry for him.

"Well, I'm sorry too, Gabe, but that's my policy. And you will need to apologize to Tess and pay for a new trophy."

He nodded and his shoulders drooped. He swiped at his eyes then straightened up and walked back into the classroom. He marched directly to Tess's desk.

"I'm sorry I yelled at you and broke the trophy. I'll get you a new one." He went back to his seat, and nobody said a word.

"Please get out your history books and read chapter seven. Once everyone has read it, we'll discuss the questions at the end of the chapter." Bella walked around the room to make sure everyone was getting out their books.

Sitting down at her desk, she got out her version of the history book and reviewed the answers to the questions, although she already knew them by heart.

When her students went outside for recess, Bella looked up Gabe's parents on her roster and punched the number listed. She may as well get it over with.

"Mitchell Smith speaking." The tone of voice was brisk and impatient.

"Hello, Mr. Smith. This is Bella Roberts, Gabe's teacher. Do you have a minute to talk?"

"Well, since you have already disturbed me, what is it?"

"We had a little problem during class today, and Gabe broke our spelling contest trophy and was rude to one of his classmates. I just wanted to make you aware."

"You're serious? You called me at work to tell me this crap?"

"Sir, this is the number I have listed to call if I need to speak to Gabe's parents. Is there another number I should have called?"

"Oh, for crying out loud, no, there is no other number. Was it an accident? Gabe usually wins that trophy. Did he drop it or something? Oh, forget it. I'll talk to him when he gets home. And don't worry. We'll replace your little trophy."

The last sentence was spoken sarcastically, followed by a click. Bella was starting to understand where Gabe's attitude came from. What a rude man. The end of the school day couldn't come fast enough.

♡

Chapter 3

BELLA PUT THE DAY behind her as she walked home. Her little house was only a few blocks from the elementary school in Missouri City, Texas. She waved at Mr. Jenkins, who was sweeping off his front porch.

"Hey, little lady," he called as she strolled by.

Bella smiled. He had called her little lady since she was eight. Some things just didn't change much over the years.

Coming to her gate, she unlatched it and strolled up the pretty little sidewalk to her front door. The house was attractive, with its blue-gray wooden siding and crisp white shutters. The roof and gutters had all been redone the year before Uncle Paul passed, and everything was neat and tidy. Tom, the yard man, kept the lawn cut and trimmed and took care of weeds. He ran the sprinkling system when needed and was willing to do anything else she needed around the house. She had planted yellow daffodils along the sidewalk, and Bella could see some buds starting to come on.

Uncle Paul had shown her how everything was handled from the time she was a teenager. He insisted that Bella learn how to look after herself. When Aunt Eleanor passed away, he and Bella did some traveling before she settled into her teaching job. Though he insisted that she never needed to work, she wanted to contribute.

When she decided to take a job at the elementary school nearby, her uncle was delighted to have her working close by and continuing to live at the house with him.

Bella and her uncle had four years of happy times together before he passed from a lung infection. She was devastated and worried she had somehow caused it. Maybe she had brought something home from school or hadn't noticed the labored breathing soon enough. It had all happened so quickly.

Sometimes Bella imagined she was bad luck for everyone who loved her. It was one of the reasons she was still afraid to date. That, and the way Bruce had treated her mom. Bella never understood why her mom let Bruce move in with them and treat them the way he did. There were so many questions she never got to ask her. She knew nothing about her father, except that he died before she was born. She had longed to have a dad who would love her and her mom and do fun things with them. And she wished desperately for grandparents she could stay with, like one of her friends had. But she didn't have a father or grandparents. And her mom didn't want to talk about it. Bella knew that her grandparents had drowned while on a cruise soon after they discovered Olivia was pregnant. She never got the chance to learn more.

Bella was her uncle's sole survivor and inherited everything, including this house. It wasn't a grand home, but she loved it exactly as it was.

She sent up a little prayer, thanking God for her aunt and uncle and all they had provided. They had taught her so much over the years. Their love had never failed her.

It was their love that had disappeared from the house.

And Bella missed it terribly.

Chapter 4

BELLA UNLOCKED HER FRONT door and went inside, excited about tomorrow's shopping trip. Harper, her best friend since grade school, had invited her to go to Rice Village, an upbeat shopping area in Texas. It would be fun to catch up and see how she was doing.

Harper was tall, slender, and dark haired, and she never stopped talking. She was the opposite of Bella in so many ways, but they had become best friends almost instantly.

She and her husband, Ben Morgan, had twin girls, Ava and Ellie, who were two and adorable. When her parents decided to move to Florida permanently, Harper and Ben had purchased the home where Harper had grown up. Bella had been thrilled that her best friend was living across the street once again.

Ben planned to take the twins to a story time at the local library so they could go shopping. He was a wonderful dad and husband and a good friend to Bella.

As she changed her clothes, she decided she would stay home tonight and get the laundry and housework done so she could enjoy the rest of the weekend. She had salad makings and could warm up some of the potato soup she had made earlier in the week to go with it.

As Bella was dusting the living room, she kept hearing a sound she couldn't identify. Was someone crying nearby? Unlocking and opening the sliding doors that led out to the small patio behind the house, she heard it again, coming from the big rose bush at the corner of the house.

She put her dusting rag inside and grabbed her jacket from the hook by the door, then made her way to the rose bush and leaned down, gently parting the thorny branches. Something moved and she jumped back. Being a bit more cautious, she leaned over and parted the branches once more, spotting a little ball of trembling brown fur. What in the world was it? Bunny or kitten came to mind, but when she scooped it up in her hands, she found a scared, very dirty little puppy staring up at her.

"Oh my goodness, you're so tiny." Bella sat on the patio chair and spoke to the puppy. "What are you doing out here all alone?" She looked around the fenced-in yard but didn't see any signs of a mama dog or other puppies.

The puppy seemed to sense that it was in a safe environment and snuggled up against her. Lifting it up, she could see the puppy was female and covered in what looked like mud, but when Bella tried to get a better look, the puppy whimpered again. Was that blood on her back?

Chapter 5

ONCE THE PUPPY STOPPED trembling, Bella took her inside. "Are you hungry? You must be cold. Did someone hurt you?" The puppy looked at her and whined.

A warm bath and examination seemed like a good start. Laundry forgotten, Bella ran warm water into the large, deep sink in the laundry room, adding a tiny bit of mild soap to make some bubbles. Carefully she set the puppy in the bath and washed her fur with the baby shampoo that Harper had left after Bella had watched the twins one weekend.

"Oh my, you aren't brown at all." As the water almost instantly dirtied, she pulled the plug and added fresh water to the bath. By the time she had repeated the process, she found herself holding a little ball of wet, curly white fur with big dark eyes. The puppy had a small abrasion on her back that seeped a little blood, but the warm water had cleaned it up, and didn't appear to be deep.

"There, that's much better, isn't it?" She wrapped the freshly bathed puppy in a fluffy pink towel, and within seconds, it was sound asleep. Bella laid her bundle gently on the couch, then called Harper, who came right over.

"Oh, she is so sweet," Harper exclaimed as soon as she saw the little dog. "I wonder if she was with the others that our neighbor, Mr. Lee, found. Someone dropped a pillowcase over the fence last night with three of them inside, but he didn't find them 'til this afternoon. He told Ben he rushed them to the vet, but none of them made it."

"Oh, that's awful. How could someone do that?"

"People are so cruel. We felt horrible that the poor little things were discarded like that. You should call the vet and see what kind they were. He's a friend of Ben's, and I have his number. His name is Anthony Fields. Actually, I can call if you like."

Bella was used to her friend rambling on, so she picked up the puppy and held her while Harper called.

After a brief conversation, she hung up. "Anthony said he could take a look at her if you want to run her to his clinic. It's just over on Elm Street, not far from the school. His appointments are done for the day, but he'll be there for about an hour."

"That sounds fine. Someone should check her out."

"I can go with you if you like. Just let me run over and tell Ben. I just fed and bathed the girls, so I'm sure he won't mind. Be right back." Harper was gone as quickly as she had appeared.

Bella carried the puppy into her bedroom and quickly switched her top for a warm sweater. Spring was here, but evenings still got cool. She picked up her little bundle and grabbed her purse, then opened the garage door just as Harper headed back across the street. The tiny dog hadn't stirred, and now Bella worried that she might not be feeling well, especially if she had been with the other puppies and somehow managed to escape.

"Here, hand her to me while you drive." Harper headed to the passenger side of the car.

"I was hoping you would drive for me. That way I can hold her."

"Okay, no problem. Already attached I see." Harper took the keys and got in the driver's seat.

"No, I'm just afraid something could be wrong if she was thrown over the fence. She has an abrasion on her back, but I didn't think it looked too bad." Bella got in and hooked the seat belt, careful not to disturb the sleeping puppy.

"Well, I guess she could have crawled out of the pillowcase and made her way across the street and under your gate. What kind of person throws away little helpless animals like that?"

"Poor baby," Bella crooned.

"Here's Anthony's office." After Harper parked, she ran around to open the door for Bella.

"Hey, Harper." The tall, lanky vet was standing in the door of his office as they walked in.

"Hey. This is my friend, Bella Roberts, and the little puppy she found. Can you tell if it looks like one of those Mr. Lee brought in earlier?"

"Bring her in and I'll take a look." He led them into the exam room where Bella gently laid her bundle on the table.

"I gave her a warm bath," Bella stated. "She was really dirty. In fact I thought she was brown at first, and she has an abrasion on her back, but she's been sleeping, and I don't know if she's okay. Will she be okay?" Bella knew she was rambling, but she was worried.

"Let's take a look." The vet stepped close to Bella and opened the towel she had laid on the table. The puppy stretched and sat up, cowering when Anthony reached for her.

"Well, she's a little smaller, but I would say she is definitely from the same litter of puppies I saw earlier today. They were brown with dirt too, and in bad shape from lack of oxygen and the impact of being thrown, probably from a moving vehicle. They appeared to be about six to eight weeks old. This one is probably the runt."

The vet continued to check the puppy over, noticing the abrasion on her back. "I'd like to keep her overnight and start an IV to get some extra fluid and nutrition in her. I can also do bloodwork and add some antibiotic if there is any sign of infection. I can tell she wasn't treated well by the way she cringes when I come near her. That will pass with some tender loving care. What are you going to call her?"

"Oh, I wasn't going to keep her, just wanted to make sure she was okay." Bella comforted the little puppy, who licked her hand.

"Well, it's obvious she prefers you over me, but I understand. I can still treat her, and you can take her to the shelter if you can't keep her. You can decide in the morning. I think she will make it. She's in much better shape than the others. The runt is usually pretty resilient."

"Will she be okay here by herself?" Bella couldn't help being concerned.

"Oh, I'll stay here with her. I have a cot in the back. We don't leave pets alone. I have an assistant who stays when I can't. She'll be in great hands. If you leave your number, I'll call in a couple of hours and let you know how she's doing." He handed Bella one of his cards.

"That would be great." Bella gave him her number and bent to give the little ball of curls a pat and whisper in her ear. "Be a good girl. I'll come back tomorrow." She turned to the vet. "Thank you, Anthony, for everything."

"No problem," Anthony said with a smile. "I'll call you later. See you around, Harper."

Bella reluctantly headed toward the door with Harper behind her.

"Hey, Bella . . ."

"Yes?" Bella turned back to see Anthony smiling at her.

"You might want to think about a name."

Chapter 6

"**COME ON, ROSIE, LET'S** go inside." Bella opened the front door as a little ball of white curls hurtled up the steps and jumped into her arms. "It's a good thing you aren't any bigger, you little minx. You'd knock me over." Smiling, she took her now-constant companion inside. She got Rosie some water, then grabbed a bottle out of the refrigerator for herself. She sat down at the kitchen table, marveling at how much had changed in the last couple of months.

Rosie had surprised everyone by her quick recovery. She had gone from a dirty, scrawny, scared little puppy to a happy, healthy ball of energy who was Bella's fierce little protector. She had weighed in at less than three pounds that first night, but at her five-month checkup last week, she had weighed a whopping six pounds. Anthony thought she would be less than ten pounds as an adult, but no one knew for sure. Looking at breeds, Anthony had Rosie listed as a Maltipoo because she appeared to have the size and stature of a Maltese but the curly hair of a toy poodle. And after looking at hundreds of pictures online, Bella was pretty sure he was right.

Anthony and Bella had become good friends, and she would always be thankful for his care and advice those first couple of months. Her friend Harper had also helped, coming over regularly to check on Rosie while Bella was at work and often took her back to her house to play. The twins loved the little puppy almost as much as Bella did. In fact, Harper and Ben were seriously thinking about getting a similar dog when the girls turned three. Ava and Ellie would be thrilled, and Rosie would have a new playmate.

Watching her little puppy drinking the cold water, Bella felt happier than she had felt since her Uncle Paul had died. A verse in 1 Chronicles popped into her head. *Give thanks to the Lord, for he is good; his love endures forever.*

"Thank you for teaching me about God, Uncle. I know you would love Rosie," Bella whispered. "Your rose bush protected her until I found her. And she is so smart. She is already completely house broken and can sit, fetch, and roll over." She sighed, knowing her uncle would have understood how attached she already was to the puppy, and knowing her aunt and uncle were in heaven looking over them.

Determined to keep her happiness flowing, she jumped up and tidied the kitchen. Now that Rosie had been outside and they'd had their morning walk, Bella was going to go through some of the boxes she had dragged up from the basement. She also needed to get busy and start decluttering the spare room. She wanted to update it to make it more usable. If only her mom were here to help. How many times had she thought that over the years?

The two years with Bruce had been a nightmare, but Bella still remembered a time when it was just her and her sweet mom. Her dad had never been in the picture, and Bella had never gotten the chance to ask about him. Her aunt and uncle didn't seem open to talking about it on the one occasion when she was brave enough to bring it up. Bella was so happy about being with them that she let it go.

Settling down on the floor of the bedroom, she pulled open the first box. Maybe she would find something about her father in their old things. She would never understand how a kind and gentle woman like her mom had ended up with a jerk like Bruce.

Rosie followed her in, making herself comfortable on the fuzzy pillow at the head of the twin bed and promptly falling asleep.

Over an hour later, Bella looked at the pile of trash beside her on the floor and felt like she was making headway. Disappointed at not finding anything about her father, she put the trash in one of the boxes she had emptied and headed outside to add it to the large garbage can sitting on the curb. The garbage service would pick up first thing in the morning, so her timing was perfect.

As she turned to go back in the house, with Rosie following right beside her, she noticed movement across the street. Thinking it was probably Ben, she turned in that direction and waved. Surprisingly, the man turned away from her, pulling the hood up on his sweatshirt and walking away.

"That's odd," she said to Rosie. "I wonder why he was in their yard."

Picking up the puppy, Bella headed into the house, thinking she would mention it to Harper the next time they saw each other.

As Bella went through box after box, the afternoon flew by. Deciding to get the closet in the spare room cleaned out as well, she opened the door and groaned when she saw everything from her uncle's room stuffed inside. Unable to get rid of anything at the time, she had put the items there when she remodeled his room. It took her another hour to unload and sort through his things, but she got it done.

Finally she pulled out a box from the top closet shelf, knowing it would be more personal stuff. Surprised at how heavy the box was, she went to work. She separated things into piles, bundled up cards that Aunt Eleanor had saved over the years, and got another box to use for photos that were intermixed with other papers. She'd have to get a photo album for all of the old photos.

She picked up an old newspaper article, startled to see it was about their accident. The picture in the article showed a little girl being carried away from the smashed vehicle by a policewoman. The article read:

> Young Woman Killed in Hit-and-Run Accident, Leaving Child Behind
>
> Saturday, April 9, 2000
>
> Olivia Ann Roberts was killed this morning in a hit-and-run accident. Her eight-year-old daughter survived and has been admitted to Mercy Hospital for evaluation. Olivia is survived by a brother, Paul Roberts, and his wife, Eleanor, who live in the area. Funeral arrangements are unknown at this time. If you have any information about the accident, please contact the police department.

The driver of the other vehicle had never been found. He had gotten away with murder.

Bella looked harder at the picture, knowing she was the little girl being carried away. There were only a couple of things she recalled clearly from the accident.

The horrendous noise of the crashing vehicles.

Seeing her mother take her last breath.

The last word her mother had whispered before she died was Bruce.

Bella had never told anyone else what she had heard, wanting to block him out forever and angry that her mother had said his name and not hers.

She put the clipping aside and shook off the trembling that had come from reading the article and continued her sorting. There were photos of her mom when she was pregnant and some of her with Bella, but no sign of anyone who might have been her father. Bella's heart ached with disappointment, but she forced herself to go on. She found a copy of the insurance policy that had matured when Bella turned twenty-one.

The insurance policy reminded her of one of the last times she had seen Bruce. Even after all these years, just the thought of him made her cringe. It was the morning of the funeral, and Bruce was talking to her uncle, telling him there was an insurance policy that should pay for the funeral, and claiming he was the beneficiary.

"I have a copy of the policy, Bruce," her uncle had stated. "Bella is the beneficiary. Whatever is left after the funeral expenses will go in trust for her."

"No way," Bruce said in a loud voice. "Olivia said she was changing that. The money goes to me." He moved toward Uncle Paul and was almost shouting in his face.

"You need to back off." Her uncle stayed extremely calm. "You'll have to provide proof of that change to my attorney. He's already handling it for Bella."

Bruce stomped off after the funeral, obviously furious. He pushed Bella into his car, scowling and cursing under his breath. Paul and Eleanor had followed them closely, watching him. Rather than taking her to get her things and something from her mom's things as he had promised them, Bruce drove directly to their house and pulled up in front of it, almost shoving her out of the car. Her aunt and uncle pulled into their driveway.

"You killed her," he had screamed at Bella, over and over. "I told her not to let you go to that stupid party."

Her uncle stepped out of the car and pulled Bella away from him and pushed her toward Aunt Eleanor who quickly took her into the house, leaving Paul to deal with Bruce.

Over her tears Bella had heard Bruce threatening them. "You won't live forever, old man. That little girl is going to pay someday, you mark my words."

Aunt Eleanor had pulled her into the bedroom and held her as she sobbed her heart out. She was too young to understand everything that was going on, but she had known two things for sure.

Her mama was gone forever. And Bruce was a bad guy.

With a shiver of fear, she put the paper away and continued her sorting. She blocked out the memories as she had done for years.

She smiled when she found a copy of her aunt and uncle's marriage license and a few more old pictures of their early years together. They were such a cute couple, right up until their last days together. After putting the pictures with the others for an album, she pulled out the last picture and stared in disbelief. It was a picture of her vet, Dr. Anthony Fields.

Chapter 7

"**WHAT IN THE WORLD.** Why would my aunt and uncle have a picture of Anthony?" The photo was a bit faded, but it sure looked like him. She looked over at Rosie who had stirred at the sound of her voice and put the picture aside.

"Okay, Rosie, I think I've had enough for one day. I need a break. It's time to see what we have for dinner." She threw the pile of trash that had accumulated into another of the empty boxes and stood up, bending over the bed to pick up the sleepy puppy.

Once she and Rosie had both finished dinner, Bella cleaned up and they headed into the living room. She turned on the television, thinking she would watch the new version of *Little Women* that had been advertised. After playing fetch with Rosie, who would fetch just about any toy she had, Bella settled the tired puppy on her lap and started the movie.

The man had stationed himself across the street again, hiding in the shadows of a large bush. He had watched Bella through her kitchen window where she sat eating and laughing about something, probably that stupid little ball of fur she called Rosie.

"Enjoy it now," he whispered under his breath. "I know you have money, and I'm going to get what you owe me."

When the lights in the kitchen went out, he was forced to move across the street and sneak around Bella's fence to her backyard. If he stood outside the corner of her fence, he could look at the back of her house. Unfortunately for him, she had closed her blinds and all he could see was a glow of light around the edges.

"That's okay, missy," he grumbled. "I'll just fix this fence while you're enjoying yourself." Careful to make sure he couldn't be seen by cars going by in the street behind him, he pulled out a heavy screwdriver and loosened the screws holding the boards of the fence. Once the screws were out, he leaned the boards against the frame, making it look like it had before. Now he could easily slip into Bella's yard to get closer.

Tired from his afternoon and evening of staking out the neighborhood, he decided to call it a night. He'd give her a chance to play nice, but first he'd scare her a bit to show he was serious. He took a long swig from the bottle in his pocket and headed back to the run-down apartment building where he was staying.

Bella enjoyed her movie, put Rosie in her little pink crate, and got ready for bed. She opened the drawer in the nightstand to put a couple of things regarding the house and property out of sight until she could file them in her little safe downstairs. As she tucked them in the drawer, she spotted the copy of the paperwork she had filed with her principal after her encounter with Gabe's father. She had tried to forget the whole thing, but the scene flooded over her like it had just happened.

The Monday after her conversation with Gabe, her students were in the lunchroom, and she was grading morning papers when someone had barged into the classroom and had slammed something down on her desk.

"Here's your trophy, Miss Roberts. Gabe was punished for breaking the other one *and* for losing the spelling contest. Does that satisfy the issue? Maybe you should be teaching your students yourself instead of pitting them against each other to win some ridiculous trophy. Good grades should be the reward for studying, nothing else."

"Mr. Smith, thank you for replacing the trophy," Bella said quietly. "I was really more concerned about the way Gabe reacted by bullying the winner and breaking the trophy. We talked about it, and I feel confident that the behavior won't be repeated."

"No worries there," Mr. Smith responded. "Gabe knows what will happen if he screws up again. I made sure of it. Just let me know if I need to beat it in a little harder." Smirking, he turned away without letting her respond and stalked out the door.

Poor Gabe, Bella had thought at the time, surprised that she was actually shaking. It had opened her eyes to why the kid had treated the other students with disregard and had a tendency to boast and bully. She made it her personal goal to help him learn a better way of communicating, and she had done it with love and kindness. She was pretty sure he wasn't going to get that at home.

It was then, as she wrote up her version of the meeting for her records, that she realized she really wasn't cut out to face the likes of Mr. Mitchell Smith. She loved working with the kids, but her experiences with Bruce had definitely scarred her. She couldn't even pretend that she liked Gabe's father and dreaded end-of-the-year conferences.

"Let love be without hypocrisy. Abhor what is evil. Cling to what is good. Romans 12:9." As Bella had spoken the verse quietly, she'd prayed she could get through the rest of the year. She had started using some of the verses she had learned with her uncle to get through difficulties. It gave her strength and always made her feel like Uncle Paul was right there with her.

She had decided to look for other work next year and forget about the principal job she had put in for. She had enough money to tide her over and could take her time finding a job that she was more suited for, one she loved. That way she could spend more time with Rosie and not have to fret about someone watching her. She'd look for a job where she could work from home or find one where she could set her own hours.

Bella closed the dresser drawer. It was time for a change.

Chapter 8

BELLA'S MINDSET AFTER THE incident with Mr. Smith didn't change. She withdrew her application for principal and started researching other jobs. She finished the year, enjoying her fourth-grade students, but stuck with her decision to leave her position.

Gabe's behavior had turned around with her encouragement and constant gentle coaching, and her conference with his parents, though a little stiff, had gone without incident. The other teachers at the elementary had thrown her a going-away party, and she was officially done and ready for the summer break.

The incident with Mr. Smith had been over four months ago, but the thought of how he had behaved still made her uneasy. She took the papers out of the drawer, tore them up, and threw them in the waste basket. No need to ever think about it again.

Once she was ready for bed, she peeked in at Rosie who was sound asleep in her crate, then crawled into her own bed.

All of a sudden, Bruce pulled her out of the room by her hair and was screaming in her face.

"Why aren't your chores done, you little brat?" His face was bright red with anger.

"Does this floor look clean to you?" He pushed her into the kitchen.

Bella could see he had spilled coffee across the tile. "No. I'll get the mop," she said, shaking. She ran for the closet, but he tripped her, and she sprawled across the floor.

"Serves you right. You aren't going to your room until your chores are done and done right." He left the kitchen.

Bella pushed herself up and got the mop. Suddenly the mop was dancing, and she was singing at the top of her lungs, "I hate Bruce; he's a goose." Over and over she sang until she was almost screaming the words.

She was laughing hysterically when she looked up and saw Bruce standing in the doorway. He lunged in and grabbed her, lifting his hand to hit her with something he was holding. It was a giant trophy, and she could read the words *spelling contest* as it came toward her face.

Sitting up abruptly, she willed the vision away, thanking God that it was only a dream. Seeing the papers about the incident with Mr. Smith must have brought back memories of Bruce. He had been so cruel to her. She had been afraid to tell her mom about the things he made her do when she was working, because he had threatened to hurt them both. And Bella was afraid that if he hurt her mom, she'd be stuck with him forever.

Shaking off the old night terrors that she had experienced for years after moving in with her aunt and uncle, she realized how far she had come from the scared little girl she had been. "I hate Bruce; he's a goose," she sang defiantly.

Chapter 9

THE NEXT DAY BELLA sat with Ben and Harper at church with a twin on either side of her, vying for her attention. Ben and Harper promised the twins ice cream after lunch if they were good.

The message was about love, especially about the love that Christ has for each of us. It reminded her of something her uncle once said when she was missing her mother.

"Love never fails, Bella," he had told her. "You know that Christ died on the cross to save us from our sins, and he loves us unconditionally. He looks after us, if we just trust in him. We feel his love all around us, always, because his love never fails."

Bella nodded, and he went on. "Your mom's love is deep in your heart, and no one can take it away. Even though your mom died, her love for you didn't. It's still around you, just like Christ's love. You just pull that inside you and hold it close, because it will never go away." He had hugged her tight, and Bella remembered feeling like she had just gotten a hug from her mother.

After church, Bella accompanied the Morgan family to their favorite little lunch spot for BLTs. It was right across the street from the church, and after eating kid-sized versions of the sandwich, the twins squealed over little bowls of ice cream—vanilla for Ava and strawberry for Ellie. Even Bella had a small bowl of butter pecan, her favorite.

They had walked to church, since it was a beautiful, sunny day. On the way home, the girls got tired, and Ben and Harper each carried a sleeping toddler. Bella unlocked the door for them, said her goodbyes, and headed across the street to her sidewalk.

Thinking about getting Rosie out for a walk, she reached to open her screen door and screamed. Frozen in fear, she stared at the white fluffy animal hanging from her doorknob with a rope tied tightly around its neck.

Ben, who had come back outside, ran over immediately, followed closely by Harper.

"No, no, no," Harper wailed. "It can't be Rosie." She put her arms around a shaking Bella while her husband reached out to remove the animal.

"It's not real," Ben said quickly. "It's a stuffed animal. Why would someone try to scare you like this, Bella? It has to be someone who knows you have Rosie."

"Rosie!" Bella shouted, hurried to unlock the door, and ran into the laundry room. Rosie yawned and stretched as Bella opened her crate. Cradling the little dog in her arms, she ran back outside. "She was sleeping," Bella told her neighbors. "Why would anyone do this?"

"I don't know, but it's a sick joke," Harper said. From the expression on her friend's face, Bella could tell that Harper was upset and angry.

"Stay right here," Ben told the girls. "I want to take a look around." He walked into the house and eventually came back outside, giving the girls a quick thumbs up. "Let me just take a quick look around the yard."

The ladies trailed around the property as Ben checked doors and windows to make sure nothing had been tampered with and peered into the garage.

"Everything looks okay. I want to go out and check the fence in the backyard." As he headed around the corner, Rosie wiggled free of Bella's arms and ran after him.

"Get back here, Rosie!" Bella rounded the corner just as Ben picked her up and handed her back to Bella.

"I'm so glad this little runt is okay, but I think you should call the police and at least let them know what happened. It looks like someone is trying to warn you or at least frighten you. It's pretty obvious that the stuffed animal resembles Rosie. Is there anyone you know of who doesn't like you or is mad at you?" Ben walked into the open garage he had just checked and threw the stuffed animal in the trash can.

"No, nobody I can think of. What kind of sick person would do something like this, Ben?"

Ben nodded at Harper who was pointing across the street, indicating she was heading home to check on the girls. "A very sick person who gets a thrill out of scaring people. Hey, what about that jerk who gave you such a hard time at school when his son broke the trophy? He was was unnecessarily rude to you. Any chance he would do something like this?"

"I don't think so, but I just don't know. It seems cruel, even for him." Bella buried her face in Rosie's soft curly fur, wanting to cry. "Thanks for checking the house and everything, Ben. You better get home. I'm taking Rosie inside."

"Glad I could help. Just call if you need anything."

Bella went inside and watched from the kitchen window. Although she felt like pulling all the shades down so no one could see into her house, she resisted. She refused to let someone scare her into hiding. Walking into the living room, she did make sure the sliding door was locked and the dowel that kept it secure was in place. She also dialed the blinds down so it wasn't easy to look in from the outside. Sitting on the sofa with her puppy, she was surprised to find that she was trembling. As she held Rosie close, Bella promised herself she wouldn't let the puppy out of her sight. She would also take Ben's advice and notify the police. Picking up her phone, she dialed the number.

Chapter 10

A WEEK WENT BY without incident, and Bella got back to her normal routine. The police department had assured her that patrol cars were driving through the neighborhood regularly, and she had actually seen their vehicles cruising by the house a couple of times.

In the meantime, she accepted a job at the local college revising online courses, which allowed her to do most of the work from home. In the fall, she would actually take on the instructor responsibilities for two of the classes. Although she missed her young students at the elementary school, she enjoyed having the extra time at home and working with a more advanced agenda. She looked forward to interaction with college students in person and online. No more parents to deal with.

She worked on her computer, set up on a little desk in the tiny dining room off the kitchen which she had turned into her office. No one had ever used the room as a dining room, preferring to gather around the table in the kitchen.

The flexibility of setting her own hours and being able to spend time with Rosie made it a perfect fit. It also allowed her to do more with Harper and her cute little twins.

Finishing up her coursework one afternoon, Bella got Rosie ready for her six-month checkup with Anthony.

As she put Rosie in her little car carrier, Bella remembered the picture she had found that looked like Anthony. She grabbed it from her dresser, slipped it into her pocket, and headed out. Driving to the clinic, she wondered again about his connection with her aunt and uncle.

As expected, Anthony gave Rosie a clean bill of health.

"She's doing fabulous," Anthony praised. "I can't believe this is the same little castaway you found just a few months ago." His assistant walked in with Rosie's six-month vaccines, and Bella got nervous about the poke that was coming for her puppy.

"Relax," Anthony told her. "She'll be fine." One little yip, and it was over. They visited for a couple of minutes, discussing the continuation of heartworm and flea medications.

"By the way, we had a little incident at my house the other day. Someone thought it would be funny to hang a stuffed animal that looked like Rosie on my doorknob."

"Maybe it was just kids playing a joke, but it's nothing to mess around with, Bella. I'm glad you notified the police. Just be careful." Anthony handed her the medication they had discussed.

As they were turning to leave the exam room, Bella put the medications in her pocket and felt the photo. "Oh, Anthony, do you recognize this picture? I found it in an old box of my aunt and uncle's I was sorting."

Taking the picture, Anthony scrutinized it. "It looks like my dad. It would have been in his younger years, of course. Why in the world would your aunt and uncle have a picture of my father?"

"I thought you might have the answer to that question. Do you know if they were friends with my aunt and uncle? Their names were Eleanor and Paul Roberts. If you see your parents in the near future, would you mind asking them?"

"Of course. No problem." Anthony slipped the picture in his wallet. "What were their names again?" He wrote the names down on a slip of paper and tucked it in with the picture. "Give me a call anytime, but Rosie looks great. I'm so glad you decided to keep her. See you both later."

Bella took Rosie to the car, placing her back in her little pink carrier. On the way home she couldn't help but think about her aunt and uncle, missing them as always and wishing they were here to talk to. She tried not to think about someone wanting to harm Rosie.

"I know you would tell me not to be afraid, Uncle, but it's easier to say than to do," Bella said aloud. "I love this little puppy so much." Trying to think of a verse that her uncle would have used in this situation, she recited one she could remember from the second book of Timothy. "For God has not given us a spirit of fear, but of power and of love and of a sound mind, chapter one, verse seven."

Still uneasy, she found herself repeating part of the verse all the way home. "God has not given us a spirit of fear. God has not given us a spirit of fear. God has not given us a spirit of fear."

Chapter 11

A COUPLE OF WEEKS went by, and when there were no further incidents, Bella started to relax again. Maybe it had just been someone playing a joke after all. Her job was going well, and Rosie was her constant companion. She could hardly wait for fall leaves, apples, pumpkins, and cute little trick or treaters.

The twins were turning three the first week of October, and they didn't know it yet, but they were getting a new puppy. Bella had gone to the animal shelter with Harper to look at one. She was about three months old and had come to the shelter after her owner had a bad accident and couldn't take care of her. She was white with a couple of big black spots on her back and around one eye. She wasn't quite as curly as Rosie, but looked similar in breed, and would make a wonderful playmate.

As Harper was driving up the street to drop Bella off, a man in a rusty, beat-up old car was backing out of Bella's driveway. He sped away in the opposite direction, squealing his tires.

"Who's that?" Harper said.

"It's probably just someone turning around in the driveway." Bella's heart was pounding, and she was already praying it wasn't another prank.

"Let me run over and get Ben. He can look around, just to be sure." Harper jumped out of the car, but stopped as Ben jogged across the street.

"Hey, ladies, who was that squealing their tires? We had a blast at the park, but the girls are worn out. They're both sleeping soundly." He stopped talking when Harper wrung her hands. "What's wrong, honey?"

"There was a man in Bella's driveway. He's the one who squealed his tires and raced away. Bella needs to go check on Rosie, but we need to make sure everything is okay first."

Bella unlocked the house, and Ben followed her inside.

"Hey, Rosie, there you are baby girl." The dog was sound asleep in her crate, but Bella took her out and hugged her tight, then hurried to check the back door and windows. She looked around, searching for anything out of place.

"Everything looks like I left it. It was probably just someone turning around. I guess I'm just paranoid right now."

"You aren't being paranoid, you're just being careful. Which reminds me, I wanted to check the fence in your backyard the other day, but Rosie distracted me, and I forgot. Let's do it now." Ben walked back outside with Bella and Rosie following.

Ben studied the fence. "I think these corner boards have loosened. I'll have to put a couple of screws in them. They probably just fell out. Let me go over and get what I need. I'll just be a minute." Ben jogged around to the front where the car was still parked. Harper had already walked across the street, so he jumped in the car and drove home.

"Come on, sweet girl. Let's go for a little walk."

They wandered around the yard until they saw Ben heading over from across the street with his toolbox. "Thanks, Ben, I appreciate it so much. I didn't realize it was even loose."

"I thought that corner looked a little funny the other night, but then I forgot all about it." Following him into the backyard, she watched as he went to the corner, pulled the boards aside, and kicked at the grass, picking up the missing screws.

"Geez, the screws fell right out, and these boards are just leaning there. Would Tom have loosened them for some reason?"

"He didn't say anything to me about working on the fence, so I don't know why he would do that." Bella swallowed hard and felt a little queasiness in the pit of her stomach. "Do you think someone else could have removed the screws?"

"I don't really know, but it's an easy fix, nothing to worry about." Ben got in his toolbox and had all the screws replaced in a jiffy. Standing back, he crossed his arms and nodded. "That takes care of it, and you can see it looks a lot better." He walked around the yard, checking the other corners. "The rest are nice and tight. I'll say something to Tom tomorrow. He's coming over to do some repairs on the playhouse for us. I can ask him to put something over those screws so they can't fall out, if you like."

"Yes, please ask Tom to do that. By the way, the puppy we looked at is adorable. The twins are going to go crazy over her. Tell Harper I'll talk to her later about what I'm bringing to the party Saturday." They waved goodbye, and Bella took Rosie back inside.

"Oh, Rosie, I sure hope someone isn't messing with us again. Why can't we just enjoy life without there always being something to worry about?" She picked up her puppy and snuggled her close. "I wish Uncle Paul were still here." A verse from second Timothy popped into her head as if her uncle were standing right beside her. She spoke the words from chapter one, verse seven.

"'For the spirit God gave us does not make us timid, but gives us power, love and self-discipline.' Then why do I feel so uneasy right now?"

She went into the spare room to wrap the presents she had gotten for Ellie and Ava. They were American Girl babies with matching outfits and tiny little teddy bears. She hoped the girls would like them. Rosie was content to lie on the floor, chewing on one of her puppy rings.

The rest of their evening was uneventful. Bella finally relaxed, playing with Rosie and working on her goodies for the party. She had called Harper earlier to let her know what she was bringing, and they were both excited to see the little girls' faces tomorrow when they saw their new puppy.

A low growl built in his chest as he stood behind the recently repaired fence. He knew they'd seen him backing out of the driveway earlier, and he wouldn't make the mistake of pulling up to her house during the day again. He had planned to put a little reminder of him in her mailbox but had to leave when he saw them coming.

Someone, probably that nosy neighbor of hers, had repaired the fence. Now he couldn't get in that way to spy on her or frighten her. He didn't dare to try standing out front when her lights were on at night, unless he hid across the street again. Maybe he should stop trying to scare her anonymously and go to the house and confront her. If she wouldn't give him the money he wanted, she'd be sorry. Her mother should have changed that policy over to him long ago, and he would've been set. That's the only reason he had hooked up with her and her brat in the first place.

Now he had waited years for Bella's stupid relatives to die, and he was determined to get his hands on Bella's money. She must have plenty. She had no one to protect her now, no one to stop him. If she resisted too much, that little puppy she seemed to adore would end up just like the stuffed animal he had left at her door. And if she wasn't smart, he just might have to plan another little accident, since she had walked away from the last one.

Chapter 12

AVA AND ELLIE'S BIRTHDAY party was a huge success. The little girls loved their babies from Bella, but the highlight of the party was the arrival of their new puppy. After running around the yard with the new dog and Rosie, they stopped to make an announcement.

"We gonna name our puppy . . ." Ava, usually the spokesperson for the twins, paused dramatically to get everyone's attention. Looking at her sister, she nodded, and they said in unison, "Smiley!"

Most of the grown-ups laughed, and Ellie held up Smiley. Sure enough, as the puppy looked around the crowd with her tail wagging and her little tongue hanging out, it seemed as if she had a huge grin on her face.

"I think that's a fabulous name," Harper told the twins. "Now let's go see your cake."

Ben had already carried the huge cake to the table. When the girls saw it, they squealed in delight.

"It's a big puppy," Ellie said. Turning, she hugged her sister and they danced around and around while their mom lit the candles.

"Okay, let's sing." Harper started singing "Happy Birthday," and soon everyone joined in.

Ava quickly blew out one candle and pushed Ellie closer and watched her blow one out. Then, holding hands, they blew out the third candle together.

"Twin magic," Harper said to the crowd. "They always seem to know exactly what the other is thinking." Smiling, she cut the cake, and Ben helped the twins carry a piece to one of the tables as the other guests stood in line.

Not a cake lover herself, Bella decided she had better find Rosie and head home. After saying her good-byes, and with a special hug for the birthday girls, she picked up her jacket and prepared to leave.

The puppies had been playing tug-of-war with one of Rosie's toys a few minutes before the cake ceremony, so Bella found the toy and picked it up. She spotted Smiley curled up under the table, chewing on the bone one of the guests had given her. Thinking Rosie had to be nearby, she searched around the yard looking under tables and chairs for the dog. Not finding her, she began to feel a little nervous and headed around to the front of the house, thinking she might have wandered toward home.

As she rounded the corner, she spotted Rosie in her yard and watched in horror as a man came around the side of the house chasing her. The dog yipped loudly as the man caught up to her and yanked her up.

"Hey, that's my dog. You put her down." Hearing Bella's voice, the little dog yipped again and tried to bite the man's hand.

"Ben, Harper, help me!" Bella sprinted toward her yard, leaping over the front yard fence where it tapered down to connect with the gate. The man threw the little dog toward Bella, jumped over the fence, and raced down the street. Terrified that Rosie might be injured, Bella ran over, picked her up, and pulled her close. The puppy licked her cheek as she checked her over.

Harper and Ben came running, with several other guests following more slowly. Looking down the street, Bella saw the man round the corner and disappear. There was something familiar about him, but she was so upset, she couldn't focus on what it was.

"There was a man chasing Rosie," Bella exclaimed. "I think he was going to steal her. What if I hadn't left when I did? I should have watched her better."

"What?" Harper and Ben both spoke at almost the same instant.

"Why would someone want Rosie?" Ben scratched his head.

"I don't know, but this wasn't kids. It was a man, and I saw him pick her up." She pushed her face into Rosie.

Harper hurried over to put her arms around Bella. "Let's go inside for a moment. Ben, why don't you go back to the party and let everyone know that Bella and Rosie are fine. I'll be over in a minute."

Bella unlocked her door, and Harper led her and Rosie inside. "I'm fine, Harper, please go back to the party."

"I'll go as soon as I know you are safe. What the heck is going on? First the stuffed animal, then the fence, and now this. I think you should let the police know what happened."

"I can call them, but if this keeps up, they're going to think I'm nuts."

"It's their job to check this kind of thing out. Just call them. I have to get back, but you're staying with us tonight. When everyone's gone, I'll come and help you bring Rosie's crate and stuff over. You can sleep in the spare room. The girls will think having you spend the night is great fun. They'll be worn out from the party, so we can talk after they go to bed. I know you have to be worried. Just lock your doors, and count on us to help you figure this out. No arguing."

Bella opened her mouth to refuse, but Harper held up her hand.

"Okay, it would make me rest easier. Thanks. Now get back to the party."

After Harper left, Bella checked all the door and window locks to make sure they were secure. Sitting in her big chair with Rosie already asleep beside her after her ordeal, Bella stared into space. "Who are you? Why are you terrorizing us?"

♡

Chapter 13

LATER THAT NIGHT, HARPER and Bella tucked the tired little girls in their beds. When they were sound asleep and the exhausted puppies were asleep in their crates, Harper, Ben, and Bella finally got a chance to talk about the mystery man.

"What kind of jerk would want to harm an innocent little dog?" Harper started out.

"Now, honey," Ben said quickly. "We don't know if he was planning to harm Rosie. What do you think, Bella? You actually saw him, right?"

"I only saw him from the side and then from the back when he ran away. I was so scared for Rosie. He just threw her down when he heard me yelling. He certainly didn't appear to be concerned about hurting her."

"Like I said, what a jerk!" Harper shook her head.

"You should think about installing security cameras, Bella. They've just come out with a system that notifies you when there is motion near your house and shows you a picture of the area. You can even have lights come on and hear any noise or voices. And you can designate a second person to get notifications. Best of all, it records the whole event. That way you have something to show the police if this man returns, and you might even recognize him. I still wonder about that kid's father who gave you such a hard time about his son and that whole spelling contest incident. You just never know what might set someone off."

Bella could tell by Ben's sharp words and furrowed brows that he was upset. "Where do I find something like that? Would they come and install it for me?"

"The electronics store over by the mall should have them. I'll tell you what, why don't we let the kids and puppies play in the morning, and you and I could run over there and check them out. And don't worry about the installation. I can always put them up for you. You'll probably need several to cover the front, back, and sides of the house. I know it will be somewhat costly, but I think you'll feel a lot more secure. I'm worried about this guy showing up some time when we aren't around. You could have me or Harper receive notifications when you do, and we would know when something is up. Would you be okay with the kiddos and dogs, Harper?"

"Of course, it's no problem at all. The girls have all of their new toys to investigate, and Smiley and Rosie can play."

"You're right, Ben. I've been worried about all this, especially since the stuffed animal incident. I would be so grateful if you'd go with me and help me decide what's needed. I'm not too worried about the cost. Sure wish Uncle Paul were here right about now, but I feel so blessed to have you guys right across the street."

Yawning, Harper came over to give Bella a hug. "That's what friends are for, honey. Now I, for one, have to get to bed. This has been a very long day."

The adults said their goodnights and headed to bed. Bella had trouble falling asleep and kept wracking her brain to determine what was familiar about the man she had seen.

"Oh, Uncle Paul," she whispered. "I miss you and Aunt Eleanor so." Trying to remember a verse her uncle might have shared with her in this situation, she came up with a one from Deuteronomy 31:6 and began to recite it. "'Be strong and of good courage, do not fear nor be afraid of them; for the Lord your God, He is the One who goes with you. He will not leave you nor forsake you.'" She tried to pull comfort from the verse. But would any security system be enough to stop this guy if he really wanted to get to her?

$\heartsuit$

Chapter 14

THE NEXT MORNING, BEN and Bella headed out right after a quick breakfast and were gone before the twins awoke. They made it to the electronics store just as it opened and identified a system with cameras compatible with Bella's cell phone.

The store manager helped them and explained how everything worked. "Once the cameras are installed, they will send a signal and audible chime to your phone and to any other phone you designate. At that point, you can view what the camera is seeing, turn on lights, hear what is going on, and even speak if you want to. You can adjust the angle and width of the viewing area any time you like, and you can also view notifications that other neighbors who have this system post. I can provide someone who can install them, but there is a charge for the service, and it will take a couple of days to get you on our schedule.

The cameras are pretty easy to install yourself, if you have someone who could help you.

"I can help her with that." Ben looked at Bella who nodded.

"Yes, I think we can get it done." Bella paid for their purchases, and they were on their way.

"Let's get this done right away," Ben said on the way home. "Harper will want to know that they are in place. I assume you will want us to get the notifications as well."

"Geez, I don't want to be that much of a burden to you guys. You've already done enough."

"It's not a problem at all. Don't be silly."

Bella and Ben went to work the minute they got back, and within a couple of hours, they had cameras installed on all four sides of Bella's house. Bella and Ben would both get a notification if there was any movement around the house or yard.

Harper and the girls had arrived earlier to supervise what they were doing, and everyone was happy with the results.

"Group hug," Harper shouted when everything was completed and the tools and ladder were put away. With Harper holding Smiley and Bella holding Rosie, they all squeezed together for a giant hug.

"You guys are amazing friends. I don't know how I'd handle all this without your support."

"Well, you don't have to. You've certainly helped us out over the years, so stop fretting. We're happy to do this. Come on, girls, we need to get Smiley home and feed her." Harper herded the twins and their little dog across the street.

Watching them go, Bella knew she was very lucky to have them. She waved goodbye, picked up Rosie, and headed inside. Harper had brought her things over and put them in her bedroom, so she put everything away, got Rosie fresh food and water, and sat down to figure out her new security system. Pulling up the app on her phone, she could actually look at each camera and see every area around her house. Satisfied that it was working properly, she threw in some laundry and settled down to look over her calendar for the coming week.

Bella took Rosie for a long walk, followed by a warm bath for Rosie and then one for herself. Not too long afterward, she headed for bed.

At two a.m., when the first notification chimed on her phone, she shot out of bed like a rocket. Shaking like a leaf, she almost knocked the lamp off her bedside table trying to turn it on. Unplugging her phone from the charger, she saw the notification and trembled as she read the message: *There is motion at the back of your house.*

$\heartsuit$

Chapter 15

WHEN THE SECURITY CAMERA footage appeared on Bella's phone, she scrutinized it to see what movement had caused the alarm. She laughed out loud when she discovered the culprit and quickly texted Ben. *Disregard notification. The bunny in my backyard has moved on to the neighbor's yard.*

When Ben replied with a text of a laughing emoji, she put her phone back on the charger and climbed into bed. Feeling relieved and satisfied that the cameras were well worth the money, she went back to sleep with a smile.

As the days went by, Bella got used to hearing the notifications on her phone and was comforted by the knowledge that no one could come near the house without setting off the alarm. Even when she was away from the house, she was still notified of any motion detected and could see what was happening via the app on her phone.

She had just finished working on grades for the students in her online class one afternoon when she got a phone call. Noticing the contact for Anthony, her vet, she closed her computer. Had she overlooked an appointment for Rosie?

"Hey, Bella, this is Anthony. I have someone in my office that I would like you to meet. Do you have time to stop over for a minute?"

"Whew! I thought for an instant that I had missed an appointment." Bella thought Anthony sounded kind of excited. "Should I be worried?"

"Of course not, just come on over."

"Well, okay," Bella answered, but Anthony had already ended the call. Shaking her head, she wondered what had just happened. Was it possible that Anthony was adding a new vet to the clinic? Or maybe he was leaving the clinic, and she was meeting his replacement. *Please, not that.* Rosie loved Anthony, and they had history together.

Stop worrying, child. Which of you by being anxious can add a single hour to his span of life? The words popped into her head as if they had been spoken out loud.

"I know, I know, Uncle. Luke 12:25." She felt silly, but years of reciting verses with her uncle made her comment as if he were standing there saying the verse to her himself. It always surprised her when she thought about how many verses she remembered. And picturing her uncle and remembering verses provided more comfort than she would ever have imagined.

A short time later, still puzzled over Anthony's call, she made her way to the clinic and pulled into the parking lot. There was only one other car in the lot besides Anthony's, but that made sense as it was already near closing time. *What in the world is going on?* Bella made her way to the door and stepped inside.

Anthony came out and greeted her, then locked the door behind her and led her to his office. Sitting in one of the extra chairs in the room was a person who looked like an older version of Anthony. The man had graying hair and was a little taller than her vet, but when he stood up to shake her hand, it was his eyes that caught her attention.

"Bella, I'd like you to meet my father, Douglas Fields."

"Nice to meet you," Bella managed to mumble as an image flashed in her brain. Suddenly she knew why he seemed so familiar to her. "Oh my goodness." Bella covered her mouth. "You're the man in the picture."

"Hello, Bella, it's so nice to meet you. Anthony has been telling me about you and your little Rosie. And, yes, I am the man in the photo you found. Did your Uncle Paul ever mention my name?"

"I don't think so." Bella was still a bit in awe of the man who resembled both the picture and his son. "You and Anthony really look a lot alike."

Anthony jumped into the conversation. "When you showed me the picture, I was pretty sure it was my dad. I showed it to him and mentioned the area where you live. He knew immediately who your aunt and uncle were. And he knew your mom. I thought you would like to meet him. I hope I didn't overstep my boundaries." Anthony spoke very fast and looked back and forth between Bella and his father.

"No worries. I knew he had to be connected to you. You look so much like him." Turning to Douglas, she spoke without hesitation. "You knew my mother? How come she never mentioned you?"

"It was a long time ago, before you were born. We were sweethearts in college but went separate ways after graduation. The night we graduated we were supposed to meet to discuss something she was upset about, but she never showed up. I tried to reach her and even reached out to your grandparents, but they told me she had gone away and changed her phone number. I took it that she didn't want to continue our relationship. It was heartbreaking, but eventually I had to let it go and move on with life."

Bella sat quietly for a moment, thoughts zipping through her mind. Her mom had been this man's sweetheart. She had been a college girl, had a boyfriend. She had never heard about any of this before. Would her mom have shared these things as she got older? Glancing up, she realized Anthony was learning about her past right along with her. He had a funny expression on his face and exchanged a questioning look with his father. She saw Douglas nod slightly.

"Bella," Anthony started tentatively. "There is something else we need to share."

Bella's stomach started fluttering when she saw the look that passed again between father and son. Why did they seem so hesitant to share more information? "W-what? Please go ahead. Did my mother do something wrong?"

Anthony walked over and sat down in the chair between his father and Bella. "Not really, Bella. She must have thought it was what she had to do. Did your mother ever mention anything about your father?"

"No, not much." The fluttering returned to her stomach. "Once I asked her why I didn't have a father like my friends, and she said he had died before she could tell him she was pregnant. She said she loved him very much and that he would have loved me if he were there. I could tell it made her sad to talk about it, so I didn't ask again. What did you mean when you said it was what she had to do?"

"When were you born, Bella?"

She raised her eyebrows but answered the question. "January 27th. What does my birthday have to do with anything?" Bella's voice came out louder than she intended.

"You were born a little less than eight months after we graduated," Douglas said softly, swallowing hard. He stood up and moved closer, leaning against Anthony's desk. "Your mom and I dated exclusively in college, and we agreed on what we wanted for the future. I was going on to school to be a doctor, and she had just gotten her nursing degree. We talked about her getting a job at the local hospital while I finished my medical degree and then traveling together as a team. One minute I thought we had a future together, and then suddenly everything changed, and she didn't want to talk about it or have anything to do with me. I think she wanted to discuss it with me that night we were supposed to get together, but something changed her mind, and she ended our relationship instead."

"What in the world!" Her heart was hammering, and she could feel the heat in her face. She jumped up and backed away from both men but stared straight at Douglas. "Are you saying that you think you might be my father?"

Chapter 16

BELLA'S HEAD WAS POUNDING. She turned away as tears welled in her eyes. She actually found it difficult to breathe. Her world was crashing in on her. Could her mom have been pregnant when she graduated and been afraid to tell Douglas? Was it possible Mom had lied to her all these years? Why would she do that? Why, why, why? There had to be some mistake, had to be an explanation. *Calm down.* She turned to face the two men.

Taking a deep breath, she tried to make some sense of it all. "There has to be some mistake. Surely my aunt and uncle would have known." Her voice sounded shaky even to her own ears, but she couldn't quite get a grip.

Anthony reached over and took her hand, pulling her over to sit back down in the chair next to him. "I think they may have known but could have been trying to respect your mom's privacy after she died."

"Knowing Olivia the way I did," Douglas added, "I think she probably felt like she would somehow ruin my plans by telling me about you. She was such a sweet, selfless person. I wish she could have shared it all with me. I was heartbroken for a long time after she left. I finished my education, but it was hard without her. It wasn't until many years later that I met Anthony's mom and was able to let it go. I don't want to burden you, but I do have some photos I would like to share with you. I don't think there will be any doubt after that about our connection. Still, we can always do DNA testing if you like."

"Can I see the pictures?" Bella was overwhelmed, but she couldn't ignore the tinge of excitement that made her hand tremble as she took the pictures that Douglas handed her. She looked down in amazement. "Who is this?"

"That's Grandma Bonnie." Anthony leaned toward her. "You look so much like her, Bella. When I first met you, there was something so familiar about you. I felt like I knew you somehow. I even told Ben and Harper about it. But I just couldn't figure it out until Dad showed me these pictures."

Flipping through the pictures, Bella saw the same woman at different ages and couldn't ignore the resemblance they shared. Finally, she handed them back to Anthony. "I see the resemblance, but I would like to have a DNA test. I have to know for sure."

"I understand. I can set that up right at my office. Today is Wednesday. How about Monday morning? Take the photos with you and think things over. I know this must be quite a shock."

"Thank you. I really appreciate that. Is there any chance we could do it tomorrow? Now that I know this much, I need to know for sure. I mean, a father . . . and grandparents . . . are your parents still alive? What will your wife think? Sorry, I have so many questions. Or at least I will, if we are related."

Douglas stood, took the pictures from Anthony, and handed them to Bella. "I have no doubt about this, and I can tell you this much. My parents are alive but don't know anything yet. My wife knows what we have discovered and is very supportive. Let's do the test in the morning. I can rush it through the lab and probably have results pretty quickly, maybe even within twenty-four hours. If it comes back that I am your father, we can get together and talk further. Does that work for you?"

Bella took a deep breath and looked at Anthony. "You could be my brother," she said in awe.

"Well, I've always wished I had a sibling." Anthony smiled. "Maybe I've had one all along. I'm glad you're willing to test right away. It's kind of exciting. Personally, I'm hoping for a sister."

Bella smiled in spite of the nerves making her stomach feel like jelly. She asked for directions to Mr. Fields's office and said a quick goodbye. Pictures in hand, she made her way outside and took a deep breath. As she slid behind the wheel of her car, tears ran down her cheeks. "Why, Mom? Why would you keep my family from me?"

When Bella arrived at home, she let Rosie out. As soon as they were back inside, she called Harper. "Hey, you won't believe what just happened. Can you come over for a minute? There is something I want to show you."

"Of course, we just finished dinner, and I am done with clean up. Ben's getting the girls in the tub. I'll just let him know then I can head right over."

"Thanks!"

When Harper arrived, Bella was sitting down at the kitchen table with six photos in front of her. "Does this remind you of anyone you know?" Bella pointed at one of the younger photos of the woman Anthony had called Grandma Bonnie.

Harper looked at the picture then looked at Bella. "Well, it resembles you, just somewhat outdated. What's going on?"

Bella blurted the whole story, trying not to sound upset. "So I could have a father *and* grandparents. And Anthony would be my brother."

"Wow. You'll know for sure once they do the DNA test, right? Why don't you just wait and see what happens. I mean, it might all be a big mistake. You know, Anthony mentioned something to Ben about thinking you looked familiar the first time you took Rosie to see him. When he told me, I thought Anthony might be hitting on you, but I told him he was probably mistaken. Jeez, I wonder if my folks knew anything about what happened back then. They knew your grandparents and, of course, your aunt and uncle and your mom."

"No worries." Bella tried to put confidence in her words. "I could have this wonderful family, or maybe not. I just want to get tested and know for sure. That's why I wanted to get it done first thing in the morning. Thinking about it all is making me crazy."

"Well, it's pretty weird, but let me know if there is anything we can do to help. Anthony? Your brother? Wow." She took one last look at the photos and shook her head. "Speaking of helping, I better get back and give Ben a hand with the twins."

They chatted a few more minutes and Harper left, still looking puzzled. Bella scooped the pictures off the table and tucked them into an envelope. She would return them tomorrow when she went for the test. She tried to push everything aside as she prepared a quick supper and made sure there was fresh food and water for Rosie.

Bedtime couldn't come fast enough. Once she was in bed, she closed her eyes and prayed. "Dear Lord, I know you'll see me through everything that's about to unfold. I believe you'll bring clarity and understanding, no matter what the DNA testing shows. Thanks to Uncle Paul and Aunt Eleanor, I know that you have always looked after me, especially after my mom died. Uncle Paul taught me how to trust in you and your love always, so tonight I place everything in your hands. Amen."

She imagined exactly what words God would use to reassure her and could almost hear him saying, "You are right, Bella. I have loved you with an everlasting love."

"Thank you, God," she whispered in the dark. "That's Jeremiah 31:3."

♡

Chapter 17

THE NEXT MORNING BROUGHT a new kind of anxiety. Bella wasn't sure if she was excited, scared, or still just plain overwhelmed. Her stomach still felt like jelly, and her head throbbed. She went through the house in a daze, bathing, dressing, taking care of Rosie, and eating a bite of breakfast. When she saw it was time to leave, she was surprised that she was ready to go.

Harper had offered to drive her, but this was something Bella wanted to do on her own. If nothing came of it, then she would put it all behind her and have a good laugh with Anthony the next time she took Rosie to the vet. And if it was true and she suddenly had a family? Well, she would have to figure that out. Her brain could not comprehend that possibility.

She followed the directions Douglas had provided and arrived at the office without any issues. Once inside the building she told the receptionist her name.

As she walked into the office, Douglas put away the patient chart he was reviewing and rose to meet her.

"Good morning, Bella. I hope you found the office without too much trouble."

"Piece of cake." She took the chair he waved her to.

"This should only take a minute," Douglas continued. "A lab technician will come in and swab both of our cheeks and take the samples of our DNA to the lab. I'm told we should have the results within twenty-four hours. Are you ready to do this?"

"Ready," Bella replied. She couldn't think past that one word.

He pushed a button on his phone, and they waited just a few minutes before someone in a lab coat entered the room.

Douglas was spot on with what he said would happen. Within a few seconds, the lab technician had swabbed both their cheeks and left the room. Bella found herself struggling for words. She couldn't quite accept the whole idea of what was happening.

"Well, I guess that's it. We should know by this time tomorrow. Are you okay?"

"Yes, I'm fine." Bella knew she was stretching the truth. Her hands were clammy and her mouth was dry. She had to get out of his office. She picked up her purse and stood to go. "Thank you for doing this. I'm sorry to be such a problem."

Douglas stood and walked with her to the door. "This isn't a problem for me at all. Worst case scenario, I get to know a friend of Anthony's and have the pleasure of meeting you. Best case, for me at least, I have a daughter. Please know that we will do what is comfortable for you either way. I'll let you know when I have the results. Does that work for you?"

"Yes, of course. Thank you." Bella walked out of the office and out of the building. Getting her keys out of her purse, she was surprised to see how hard her hands were trembling.

"Good grief," she told herself. "Pull yourself together."

Returning home, she took her purse into the bedroom. As she placed it on the dresser she noticed the photos were still inside the front pocket. She would have to give them back to Anthony or Douglas another time.

Bella went about her daily routine, trying to lose her thoughts in the class she was teaching. She returned emails to several students and put together an outline for their next project. After lunch, she took Rosie for a leisurely walk around the neighborhood and did a couple of loads of laundry. She tried to not think about what the test results might reveal.

After a light supper, she gave Rosie a bath and had just finished brushing Rosie's soft, curly fur when the phone rang.

It was Anthony calling. Her mouth went dry. She ran her tongue around the inside of her cheek and tried to answer normally. "Hello, this is Bella."

"Bella, this is Anthony. Would you be willing to run over to Dad's office? The lab just dropped off the results of your DNA testing, and he would like us to both be there when he opens it." Bella could hear a trace of anxiousness in Anthony's voice.

Bella eyes widened, and her stomach did another somersault. She said the first thing that popped into her head. "No way, he can't have the results this fast."

"Well, I'm sure they gave it priority since he's right there in the building. I could tell from his voice that he's nervous, and I think he wants us all to know at the same time. Can you make it?"

Was it really possible that Anthony was her brother? "Um . . . sure. Let me just get Rosie in her crate, and I'll be right over."

"You can bring her, if you like."

"That's okay. She just had a bath and it always makes her sleepy, so a little time in the crate will be fine. See you soon." She clicked off her phone and went to get Rosie a treat and get her settled in the crate with a warm towel.

"I'll be right back, sweetie." Bella grabbed her purse and headed out the door.

As she was driving to the office, she thought about all of the years with her aunt and uncle. She wondered if there was any way they could have known about Douglas and kept it from her, and she found herself talking to Uncle Paul as if he were sitting beside her.

"Did you know about Douglas, Uncle? Did you know they were sweethearts in college and were planning a life together? Did you like him? Why didn't mom tell me about him? Why didn't you? Is there a chance that he could be my father? Did mom swear you to secrecy?" She didn't want to think her uncle might have kept something like this from her. She wanted to trust God with all her heart. So she came up with her own verse and recited it. "'For I am persuaded that neither death nor life, nor angels nor principalities, nor powers, nor things present nor things to come, nor height nor depth, nor any other created thing, shall be able to separate us from the love of God which is in Jesus Christ our Lord,' Romans 8:38–39. I am not going to worry, because God has my back, no matter what the future holds. That is what my uncle would want me to remember." She smiled at the silliness of talking to herself and kept right on doing it. "It's going to be okay. I know that no matter what, God's love will not fail me."

She pulled into the office parking lot and parked. She was about to find out if she was related to the Fields family. She was about to discover whether or not she had a biological father, brother and grandparents. It could be true, and the family she had always dreamed of could be waiting to welcome her. Or, it could all be some kind of crazy mistake. Taking a deep breath, she opened the door and headed out to face her future.

Chapter 18

BELLA MADE HER WAY inside the building and to the door that led to his reception area. Anthony was there waiting for her. He led the way to his dad's office, and Bella was surprised to see a woman sitting with Douglas.

Anthony explained. "Bella, this is my mom, Helen."

"It's good to meet you, Bella," she responded quietly.

"I hope you don't mind, Bella. I thought Helen should be here too. Okay, let's get to these results, shall we?" Douglas waited until Bella and Anthony were sitting across from him and his wife before he tore open the envelope. He quickly scanned the results and passed them to Anthony.

Anthony and Bella put their heads together and looked at the results at the same time. All Bella could really focus on was the underlined number: 99.9 percent match.

Anthony read the line of text after the number aloud. "'The analysts' calculations put the probability of paternity for the tested man at 99.9 percent. We therefore consider that man to be the biological father of the child.'"

Bella felt the blood drain out of her face as reality washed over her.

"Are you okay?" Douglas looked at her with raised eyebrows, and walked around to the front of his desk where he sat against the edge rubbing his hands up and down his thighs.

Before she could reply, Anthony reached over and took her hand. "Bella, you're my sister. It's true. You're really part of our family."

"I-I don't know what to say." Letting go of his hand, she glanced around the room at the three faces looking back at her and saw nothing but delight in their expressions. Astonished that they would be so excited to have her join their family, she spoke without thinking. "Are you glad?"

Douglas pulled an extra chair up to Bella's and took both her hands in his. "Honey, I was already pretty sure about these results. Your resemblance to my mother is uncanny. The pieces that were missing all those years ago finally fell into place when Anthony showed me the picture you found and told me how familiar you seemed to him. I'm just really sorry that I didn't know before, when your mother died. I hope you will give me a chance to get to know you now. Still, if you need time to think about it, we'll all understand. We won't push you if it's not what you want."

Bella quickly pulled her hands away and peeked at Helen who was smiling as well. She stood and came over to stand near Anthony and his dad. "I can see the question in your eyes, Bella, and I want to put your mind at ease. This is not difficult for me at all. I know all about Douglas and Olivia, and I know that he loved your mother very much. But it was a long time ago, and we have been blessed with a deep love and a wonderful marriage. Anthony is our pride and joy, but unfortunately, additional children were not in the cards for us. However, to discover you and have a chance to add a daughter to our family? Well, that would be nothing short of a miracle."

Bella searched Helen's face and saw nothing but sincere kindness staring back at her. Was it really possible that after all these years she was part of a family like the Fields? She knew what a great friend Anthony had already become, but her brother? It just didn't seem possible. And to have a dad now, after all this time? Uncle Paul had been a wonderful uncle, but a real dad? She just couldn't believe it.

"I don't know what to say. I'm overwhelmed by your desire to add me, a total stranger, to your family. I need to absorb this and figure out what it all means."

"Of course you do, and I'm sorry we're finding this out so late in the evening. I couldn't wait to have my suspicions confirmed, and I wanted you all to be here. Let's call it a night and take a few days to decide what to do with this information. It's really up to you, Bella, to decide how to move forward." Douglas's voice wavered a bit as he finished.

Helen glided easily into the conversation. "What would you say to coming over to our house on Saturday and discussing this further? We could have some lunch and figure out what's next." Helen was holding hands with Douglas as she issued the invite, and he nodded his agreement.

"I could pick you up," Anthony chimed in. "That way you would know the way in case you want to come again. And you could bring Rosie. Right, Mom?"

"Of course. We heard about you rescuing that puppy. We'd love to meet her."

Their enthusiasm was contagious, and Bella found herself agreeing to have lunch with them on Saturday. "Well, I'd better get home before it gets any later." Bella stood and Anthony followed, offering to walk her to her car.

"I know this has got to be overwhelming," he told her on the way. "But, honestly, you can trust my parents. They would never hurt you or push you into anything you don't want. And I won't either. I can stay your friendly neighborhood vet or become your big brother."

He gave her a soft punch on the shoulder. "Come on, you know you want a big brother like me, right? Even though you *are* older than me."

While Bella knew from the tone of his voice that Anthony was teasing her, she also knew from past conversations that he had always longed for a sibling. She had to get home and think all this through. Her head was spinning, and she didn't know what to think or say. She certainly didn't want to hurt Anthony's feelings, so she tried to keep it light. "You're silly. I better get going. Do you want to pick me up about one o'clock? Are you sure it's okay to bring Rosie?"

"Yes and yes. I will be there promptly at one o'clock. Drive careful. See you soon." With those words, he turned and headed back toward the building just as his parents were coming out. She watched as they all hugged, then stood around talking.

As she drove home, she couldn't help but feel a twinge of excitement thinking about the possibilities. She had a real family to share the rest of her life with. All she had to do was say the word and she would become one of them. She didn't know if it would be as easy as they made it seem, but she did have the advantage of already knowing Anthony and considering him a good friend. It all felt like a dream come true. She had father who wanted her, and a brother, and maybe even grandparents. "No way," she said out loud. "No possible way!"

Chapter 19

DISTRACTED BY THE EVENTS of the day, she didn't notice the car following her until it pulled into her driveway behind her. She left the garage door open. Seeing lights on across the street, she knew that Ben would get the same notification she had just heard on her own phone: *motion in the driveway.*

As a man stepped out of the car and came toward her, Bella purposely flipped on the garage light and stood where she could be seen. The hairs stood up on the back of her neck, but seeing the front door open across the street, she knew that either Ben or Harper was watching.

The man looked old, and she got the same feeling that she had gotten the day of the twins' birthday party when she had seen the man pick up Rosie and throw her down. She was pretty sure this was the same man. He seemed so familiar, but she couldn't place him until he spoke.

"Well, look at you, all grown up and purty as a peach. I bet you think you're somethin', don't cha? Where's that little puppy dog you're so fond of? Almost lost her, didn't you?"

"Bruce." In shock, it was all she could manage to say.

He stepped forward and grabbed her by the arm. "Let's me and you go inside and have a nice little chat, missy. There's the matter of a little money you owe me."

Shaking off his hand and heading past him toward the street, Bella found strength from the figures she saw stepping out on their front porch. "Get out of here, Bruce," she said over her shoulder. "I have nothing to say to you. I don't owe you a penny."

Harper and Ben had made their way to the edge of the street, and Bella headed toward them. She was more thankful than ever for the security system that had alerted her neighbors.

Turning, Bruce snarled. "Another time, missy!" He jumped into the same beat-up vehicle that she and Harper had seen in her driveway and sped away.

Shaking like a leaf, Bella almost ran into Harper's arms. "It was Bruce!"

"Bruce? You mean the Bruce who lived with you before the accident? You have to be kidding me."

"I wish I was." Now that he was gone, Bella gained some composure, then she quickly lost it again as she thought about everything that had happened. "Oh, Harper, what am I going to do?"

"Let's go back to your house and sit down for a minute."

Ben gave his wife a quick kiss on the cheek, then made an excuse to check on the kids. Harper and Bella walked across the street and went into the garage. She unlocked the back door and rushed inside to get Rosie. Bella brought Rosie out to do her business, then picked her up and hugged her tightly as she went back inside. She watched from the kitchen as Harper closed the garage door, turned out the light, and followed them inside.

Bella mindlessly got fresh water for Rosie and plopped down at the table where her friend was already seated. "There's so much I have to tell you. The Fields really are my family, and the DNA test confirmed it, and now Bruce is back. I hate that man!"

"Start with the DNA testing. Did you get the results already?"

"Yes, tonight. I was just getting home from Anthony's father's office when Bruce pulled in my driveway. Oh my goodness, Harper, he must have been following me or waiting near the house. I was so distracted by everything I found out tonight, I was in a daze. I wasn't paying attention. He could have gotten in the house."

"Okay, let's make some tea, and you can start from the beginning." Familiar with Bella's kitchen after years of coming and going, Harper got up and gathered cups and tea. She heated water, placed their favorite tea bags in each cup, and returned to the table. "Now spill."

"Okay, well, Douglas, Anthony's father, he's a doctor, did you know that?" Bella couldn't stop herself from sidetracking.

"Yes, I knew. Go on."

"Okay, sorry, my mind is all over the place. Well, Douglas rushed the test and got results late today. He wanted me and Anthony to be there when he opened them. Oh, and his wife was there too. Helen was her name." Seeing her friend nod, she went on. "Anthony and I read the results, and honestly, all I really saw was the 99.9 percent. That means he's my father." Bella was still having a hard time believing it herself, so she wasn't surprised when Harper put her hand over her own mouth, and her eyes got big.

"Are you kidding me? Anthony's really your brother? Well, I'll be darned."

"I know. It's weird, right? Apparently Douglas and my mom dated in college and had a future all planned. Then right after graduation, they were supposed to meet, and my mom never showed up. Douglas told me he never saw her again. It took him years to get over her. When Anthony showed him the picture I found in Uncle Paul's things and told him about me and how I seemed familiar to him, he said everything fell into place." Bella took a breath and swallowed hard, but rushed on.

"He thinks she was upset about the pregnancy and didn't want to ruin his career or something. She wouldn't return his calls, changed her number and everything, and just disappeared. He tried to reach out to her parents, but a few months later, they went on a cruise and drowned. I know that part's true because I remember my uncle and mom talking about the cruise. My mom thought they went because she had shamed them by getting pregnant, but Uncle Paul told her it wasn't true. I don't know, Harper, it all seems crazy to me."

"Wow," was all Harper could say. "Wow, wow, wow!"

"Now you know why I was so distracted that I didn't see Bruce behind me. What am I going to do about him? He says I owe him money. I think he's talking about the insurance policy that my mom had. I was the beneficiary, but I think he tried to talk my mom into changing it to him. Obviously she didn't, but he thinks I owe him. I'm not giving him any money."

"Of course you're not. That man is disgusting. Do you think he's the one who has been terrorizing you?"

"I do. He's much older of course, but he looks like the man I saw in my yard. I knew he was familiar, but I couldn't place him until I heard him speak. I'll never forget that creepy voice. You have no idea how mean he was to me when he lived with us. He was always watching me and doing things to make me look bad. One time he even took me to this old barn outside of town and made me sit on the floor in the corner while he worked on this old pickup truck. I was scared to death. I even saw a rat.

"I think my mom was getting ready to kick him out when we had the accident. I never understood why we all moved in together in the first place. He didn't even seem to like her that much, and he hated me."

"Oh, Bella, that had to be awful."

"It was. He was so scary, and he's really mean. Do you think I should call an attorney and try to get something in place to keep him away from me?"

"Yes. Hey, did you think to look at the security camera to see what was recorded? That would give you proof that he was here, maybe even the threatening part. I think it records voice as well as picture."

"Yes, it does. I had that included. Let's look." Taking out her phone, Bella pulled up the recent driveway video. "Here it is."

The girls watched the video and saw Bella pull up into the garage, followed closely by another vehicle. They watched and listened as Bruce got out of his car, and Harper's mouth dropped open in amazement when she saw Bruce grab Bella's arm and heard his threatening words to her.

"Oh, Bella, this is proof he's threatened you. You need to try to get in to see your attorney first thing tomorrow morning and get a personal protection order against this creep. I mean it. Don't even hesitate."

"No, I won't. That man scares me to death. Oh, Harper, I'm so confused and overwhelmed right now.

This is so much to take in. I mean a father and a brother, and maybe even grandparents? It all seems unreal to me. And now this creep Bruce is around again, trying to ruin everything. I thought he was out of my life for good. I'm so tired, I can't even think straight."

"Why don't you just lock up and go to bed? We can talk again tomorrow, and I promise this is all going to get sorted out. Call and see if you can get that appointment. Tell them you're in danger, and it's an emergency."

Harper stood and took care of her teacup. "And by the way, having someone like Anthony for a brother might not be all that bad. And a doctor for a father, well, it could certainly be much worse. Now lock up so I know you're okay, and get some sleep."

Bella followed Harper to the front door and said good night, letting Rosie out one more time while her friend looked on. After the puppy was back, she closed the door, locked it, and looked out the window to wave her friend home. Then she dropped the curtain and fell heavily into the chair where they had been sitting.

After a few minutes, she dragged herself out of the chair and went through her nighttime routine. At the last minute, she decided to take something the doctor had prescribed to help her sleep. She already dreaded what the next day might bring. Just thinking about that creep Bruce made her tremble.

Chapter 20

BRUCE WASN'T DONE WITH Bella, not by a long shot. He'd have to move fast if he was going to get the money she owed him. He had figured out the security setup when those neighbors of hers had arrived so quickly on the scene. There were ways to get around that. He knew someone who could hack those systems easily. It had taken a threat or two, but if the man knew what was good for him and his little girl, he was already working on it. As soon as Bruce knew they were disabled, he had a little surprise in store for miss high-and-mighty Bella Roberts. If she didn't cooperate, that little dog of hers would have a very short life indeed.

He gathered what he needed into a black backpack. Bruce was pretty happy with himself at the moment. This was a better plan in the long run. He put the backpack and the few boxes of belongings he owned in the trunk and left the dumpy apartment he had rented under another name. He'd have plenty of money to move on to another place when Bella paid him what she owed him. The insurance policy was $500,000, and he intended to get every penny of it. She didn't need it anyway. He should have had it long ago. His original plan to get rid of her hadn't worked, but he'd get that money one way or another.

Driving outside of town, he returned to the ancient barn where he had left the old truck since the accident. The man who had paid him to look after the barn had died years ago, and as far as he knew, he had no relatives. The truck had sat for all these years right under the cops' noses.

There was a dirt path that led out to the barn, and the weeds had grown up on both sides past the top of his car. The bushes and weeds scratched at the sides of his vehicle, but he pushed on. He didn't care. He planned to buy a brand-new vehicle as soon as Bella turned over the money to him.

He pulled up to the barn and went in the side door that he had to force open. He felt his way to the lantern that was on top of a crate in the corner, he reached in his pocket for the lighter that he used for his smokes. He lit the lantern and looked around.

The rusted old truck was far worse than he remembered, and the accident hadn't helped. The bumper that had smashed into Olivia's car had fallen off. It had barely stayed attached until he got the truck back in the barn after the accident all those years ago. He decided he might just let the lantern tip over accidently when he left for good. He didn't want anything left behind that Bella could use against him. She was lucky he wasn't leaving her inside to burn. But he wanted her around in case he ran out of money. If this worked as well as he thought it would, he could always come back for more.

The phone in his pocket vibrated.

"It's done. You won't have any trouble with the cameras notifying her. She won't even know they're not on. Now leave me and my family alone."

"Just hold your horses, Gus. I have to get the money first. I'll contact you as soon as I have it. Then you and your daughter are in the clear."

Bruce chuckled as he clicked off the phone. People were so easy to manipulate. One little threat to hurt his daughter, and the man had cowered. The fool should have told him to get lost, but he wasn't as smart as he thought he was.

With one last look around, he was satisfied that everything would work just the way he had planned. He turned off the lantern and made his way back outside.

From the trunk, he pulled out the black backpack with the things he needed and put it in the front seat. He hoped the dog wouldn't wake Bella before he could get to her, but he had a piece of grilled meat in the bag he had doctored with a sedative. He was pretty sure it would keep her busy 'til it knocked her out.

Back in the car, he was beyond excited. Nothing thrilled him more than getting the best of someone who thought they were better than him. Even as a kid, this girl had been nothing but trouble, and he was finally going to make her pay. She wouldn't get her way this time, and no one was going to be around in the middle of the night to rescue her. He might be twenty years older, but he was lean and mean. He'd been lifting weights for months at the run-down room the apartment complex called a gym. Well, it was good enough to strengthen his muscles to handle the little brat, just like he had years ago. Besides, she wouldn't take a chance of losing her dog. Nope, he had everything covered.

Whistling, he turned onto the highway and headed back toward town.

Chapter 21

BELLA WAS SMOTHERING. THERE was something over her nose and mouth and she could barely
breathe. She could feel herself dragged out of bed and
pulled across the room, but everything was fading fast.
Then she heard his voice.

"You make one sound and that dog of yours is dead,
do you hear me?"

Bruce.

Where was Rosie?

Bruce pressed the dirty kerchief into her mouth,
choking her. She nodded and tried to clear the cobwebs.
It was dark in the house except for a small nightlight she
left on in the hallway, but she saw Rosie in her crate as
Bruce pulled her into the living room.

He quickly tied Bella's hands behind her back then
shoved her out the sliding door into the backyard. He

held tightly to the rope that secured her hands with one hand and carried Rosie's crate in the other.

He led her to the farthest corner of the backyard, opposite the corner that Ben had repaired. He had loosened the boards in this corner now and shoved her through hard enough to knock her down, chuckling as he put the boards in place behind them. He yanked her up by the rope, then hurried to a car parked on the street behind Bella's house. Setting the crate down again, he shoved Bella into the front seat and buckled the seatbelt around her. He put the crate in the back seat, took off the black backpack and threw that in as well, got in, and sped away.

"Well, bet you didn't expect to see me again so soon, did you?" He reached over and pulled the kerchief out of her mouth.

"Please, Bruce, don't hurt Rosie."

"'Please, Bruce, don't hurt Rosie,'" he mimicked sarcastically. "Just shut up!" He grabbed another rag out of his pocket and shoved it in her face.

Bella slumped over and everything went dark.

When she came to, she was sitting on the floor in the middle of a pile of hay. Her hands and feet were both tied now, but at least the rag was not across her mouth and nose and hung limply around her neck.

There was fuzzy light from a candle—no, a lantern—in the corner, and Rosie was lying in her crate a few feet away. She wasn't moving. Bella's heart stopped for a minute until she focused on the dog's little chest rising and falling and realized she was sleeping. Relieved, Bella pushed up into an awkward sitting position against the hay just as Bruce strolled in through a rear door. Bella could see the sun was rising in the morning sky in the split second he closed the door.

"Well, well, well. It looks like the little lady is finally awake. Did you sleep well? I guess the chemical I used was a little strong. Thought it might have killed you. Lucky for me, you're still kicking."

"What day is it? How long did I sleep? Where am I?" Bella tried not to sound as terrified as she felt.

"If you must know, it's Saturday, and you've been sleeping for over twenty-four hours. Lucky for you, I had some shopping to do. Now, are you ready to have that little chat I mentioned earlier, or do I have to convince you that it's in your best interest, or shall we say, your little doggy's best interest?" He kicked Rosie's crate and woke her up abruptly.

Rosie turned toward Bella and whined.

"What do you want? Why have you come back after all these years?"

"I came back for what's mine, and you know it. Just like I told that uncle of yours, I was supposed to be the beneficiary of that insurance policy. Olivia promised me she was going to change it. I want the money, and

I know you have plenty. Just give me the $500,000 and I'll disappear."

"You must be crazy! I was the beneficiary of that policy from the start. My mom wouldn't have changed it. It was insurance in case anything happened to her, which it did. When that truck crashed into us and killed her—" Bella stopped midsentence as she had finally adjusted to the dim light and realized what she was seeing.

Parked on the other side of the barn was the truck. It was rickety, rusted, and falling apart, but it sure looked like the truck she remembered from the accident.

"I-Is that the truck that crashed into us?"

The twisted smile on Bruce's face made Bella wish she had kept quiet.

"You just shut your mouth," he snarled. "I don't know what you're talking about." He stalked over to her and leaned down until his foul breath was in her face. "I have one more detail to take care, so you only have couple of hours left to figure out how to get me my money." He kicked Rosie's crate again. "Otherwise, this precious little mongrel of yours dies." Bruce slammed the door on his way out of the barn.

Chapter 22

BELLA COULDN'T STOP THE tears that ran down her face. She managed to scoot herself over to Rosie's crate inch by inch. Once there, she turned so her hands were up against it behind her and was rewarded with a little tongue licking her through the crate bars.

"Oh, Rosie," she wailed. She knew she was going to have to give Bruce the money or he would kill Rosie.

She studied the truck again, certain it was the one that had come up beside her all those years ago and then crashed into them when her mom swung the car around.

An image of the accident flooded into her head. She remembered unbuckling her seat belt as the truck sped away and leaning over the front seat where her mother lay crumpled over the steering wheel. She'd screamed for her to wake up, but the last sound that had come from her mother's mouth was, "Bruce." Bella remembered the soft whisper and had watched as her mother took her last breath.

At the time, and even in later years, she was hurt that his was the last name Mom had uttered. Shaking her head to clear the image, another thought surged.

"She was trying to tell me that it was Bruce!" At Bella's exclamation, Rosie whimpered. "Sorry, Rosie. We have to find a way to get out of here." She gazed around the barn for anything that would cut the twine that was tied around her wrists and ankles.

An old hand saw hung low on the wall. Bella scooted one painful inch at a time until she reached the wall. She lay on her side and kicked as hard as she could to knock the saw to the floor. It seemed to take forever, but she finally connected, and the saw moved a little. Exhausted, she turned onto her stomach to look at Rosie who was whining softly.

"It's okay. I'll get it down and get us out of here." She kicked and kicked until sweat ran down her back.

Just when she was about to give up, she heard her mother's voice. "*I love you, Bella, I'll always love you. You can do this.*"

Bella gave one last kick with all her might, and her foot connected with the saw. The rusted nail gave way and the saw tumbled, almost on top of her. She rolled away and rested a minute to catch her breath, then tried to manipulate her body to get the saw between her arms so she could try to cut at the twine securing them.

Her arms were scratched and bleeding from both the straw and the saw, but after what seemed like dozens of attempts, she had the saw near the twine. She scooted back to the wall and managed to get to her knees and leaned against it until she felt the saw pressed against the twine. With slow, careful moves, she began the task of rubbing the twine against the saw.

The sweat was running into her eyes now, blurring her vision, and she wanted to quit. She blinked to clear her sight. All of a sudden, she saw her mom and aunt and uncle right in front of her, holding hands and trying to tell her something. She strained forward, blinking hard, and thought she heard *"Love never fails, Bella."* The vision floated away. Shaking her head, she tried to draw the vision back, but it was gone.

Bella lay on the floor and wept. Once she was spent, she tried to sit up again and noticed that her hands were not as tightly bound as before. With the help of the saw, she had loosened the twine. Immediately she scooted back over and continued working the twine against the saw. She heard a small tearing sound and felt the twine loosen. She had to keep going. Finally the twine broke, and she tipped over in surprise.

She quickly severed the ties at her feet and stood shakily. Moving over to Rosie's crate, she opened the door and hugged her. Rosie licked her face frantically, shaking all over. Determined to get the dog out of the barn, Bella put Rosie back in the crate and started toward the door.

As she got close, she could hear pounding footsteps. She quickly ducked around and back behind the old truck, just as the door came crashing open.

Chapter 23

ANTHONY KNOCKED ON BELLA'S door promptly at one o'clock on Saturday. Finally he decided to go across the street and see if she was visiting with Ben and Harper. Ben was outside with the new puppy and waved as Anthony came across the street.

"Hey, Anthony, what's up?" Ben shook his friend's hand.

"I was supposed to pick Bella up. Do you know where she is?"

"I think she's home. I haven't heard her security system go off, so she must be. Otherwise I would have gotten a notification that there was motion in her driveway when she left."

"I've been pounding on the door, but she doesn't answer. I was supposed to pick her up for a family dinner."

"That's so weird." Ben laughed. "I mean to think of you as her brother."

"Can you just check the security system, funny guy? I'm worried."

"Of course, come on in and I'll check." Ben went inside with Anthony close behind him. He checked his phone for notifications. "See, I told you. Nothing. She has to be home." He hollered into the kitchen. "Harper, can you call Bella? Her *brother* is worried about her." Chuckling, he pounded Anthony on the shoulder as Harper walked in dialing her phone.

"Well that's weird," Harper said. "I know she had a lot going on yesterday, and I had every intention of talking with her, but Ellie wasn't feeling well, and I got distracted. I should have checked on her. She was pretty overwhelmed by all that was happening."

She peeked out the window at Bella's house. "Still, I know she was excited about going to your parents' for lunch. Let me get the spare key she gave me. I'll peek in on the twins, then we can go over and make sure everything is okay. Did you see her take Rosie out this morning, Ben? You should have gotten a notification on your phone."

"Well, I already checked, and there aren't any on there since two nights ago. You're right, though. There should have been something by now."

Harper left and was back in a flash. "The twins are both sound asleep. Let's go."

"I'll stay here in case they wake. You and Anthony go check it out."

Within moments his wife was running back in the front door, with Anthony on her heels.

"She's gone! Call 911! Something's wrong!"

Ben put an arm around Harper's shoulders and tried to calm her. "What are you saying, honey, what's wrong?"

Anthony was frantic as well and jumped into the conversation. "Her bed's a mess, and it looks like somebody dragged her out of it! And the sliding door was open."

"Rosie's gone too," Harper added. "And her favorite toy was tossed next to the washing machine. Rosie always sleeps with that toy. Bella even has an extra one in case anything happens to it. Something's wrong, Ben, I know it."

"Okay, okay, I'm calling the police."

As Ben dialed 911, Anthony stepped outside and made a call on his cell phone.

"Hey, Dad, something has happened to Bella. The police are on their way. Okay, see you soon." Anthony walked back inside. "My dad is on his way over. I'm heading back over to Bella's to meet him there."

"The police said not to touch anything. They will try to dust for prints. I bet it's that creep, Bruce. He wasn't happy with us interfering the other night. Come on, Anthony, I'll go with you. I can fill you and the police in on Bruce. Don't worry, Harper. We'll find her."

Harper nodded, but Ben could see tears in her eyes.

Anthony waited until the door closed and questioned Ben before he could open his mouth. "Who's Bruce, and why would he want to harm Bella?"

Ben filled him in as they walked over to Bella's. "He was here a couple of nights ago trying to bully her. I got the notification from her security system, and Harper and I came out and scared him off. He must have done something to her security system and returned."

Anthony heard sirens, followed closely by the police car pulling into Bella's driveway. Ben gave the officers the information he had about Bruce, and Anthony told them what he and Harper had discovered when they checked the house. The officers went inside. Ben and Anthony followed as the policemen searched the backyard and discovered the spot where someone had gone through the fence.

As they came around to the front of the house, the woman who lived next door came over. "Is there a problem with Bella? I saw that man pushing her around and throwing her dog in the back seat of his car late last night. I was hoping it wasn't as bad as it looked, but I wrote down his license plate just in case. It's right here on this envelope. It was an old beat-up Honda Accord, and I think it was white or gray, but it was awfully dirty." She handed the policeman the envelope, visibly shaken.

Ben walked over and put his arm around her to steady her. "Thank you, Mrs. Watkins. That was really smart. I'm sure it will help Bella."

One of the cops nodded. "Officer Curtis is calling it in right now, and yes, that's going to help us find her. Thank you, ma'am. I'm Officer Harry. If you think of anything else, give me a call." He handed his card to Mrs. Watkins, and both officers disappeared back inside.

Anthony's dad pulled up in front of Bella's house and jumped out. "What's happening, son?"

Anthony quickly filled his dad in on what he knew.

The policemen came out the front door, and Officer Curtis walked over and shook hands with him. "Good afternoon, Doctor. How do you know Bella Roberts?"

"Nice to see you on the job instead of in my office," his dad replied. Bella's my daughter, and we have just reconnected after many years. What are you doing to find her?"

"We have the license plate of the car she left in, and we're doing our best to locate it. We've secured the house and need everyone to stay away from the residence at this time." The officer's radio went off just as he finished the sentence. "This is Officer Harris. Yes sir, we're on our way." He turned to the other officer. "They've spotted the car heading out of town. Let's go, Harry." Jumping in the car, they backed out of the driveway and sped off.

The three men looked at each other, nodded, and jumped into the doctor's car without saying a word. Anthony drove, following the direction of the police car's screaming siren.

Chapter 24

BELLA WATCHED IN FEAR as Bruce sprinted inside. When he saw that she was gone, he started cursing and raced around looking for her. She tried to slink around the truck so he wouldn't see her, but Rosie spotted him and started barking.

"You stupid woman!" he shouted. "Your time is up. We're leaving right now. And that mutt can stay right here. You can come and get her after you give me the money."

Bella's heart was pounding with fear and anger, but she put Rosie down and walked around the truck to face Bruce. "I'm not giving you anything, you horrible excuse for a man." Bella's emotions were out of control, and she was shaking and screaming at him. "I know it was you who killed my mother. We'll see what the police have to say about that." She was so upset, she didn't see the blow coming until it knocked her to the ground.

"Just shut up!" Bruce snarled. He grabbed her arms and dragged her over to where the rope lay in the hay, and had her wrists secured behind her again before she could recover from the blow. "You will give me the money." He jerked her up and shoved her toward the door, knocking her down again. Almost dragging her, he came to an abrupt stop.

Four police cars surrounded his car and half a dozen armed policemen stood with their guns pointed in his direction. Bruce pulled Bella in front of him and slowly backed into the barn. Then he shoved her aside, ran for the other end of the barn, and slipped through an opening in the back at a dead run.

Bella managed to get up as several officers ran in the door.

"He went out the back!" she yelled. Watching them follow in the direction Bruce had gone, she slumped against the rusty truck in relief.

Before she could catch her breath, Anthony, Ben, and Douglas rushed into the barn.

Ben hurried over when he saw her. "Oh my gosh, are you okay?" He pulled out a small jackknife and severed the twine holding Bella's wrists behind her.

Anthony grabbed her as she stumbled forward, holding her like he would never let her go. "Oh, sis."

He almost sobbed. "I thought we might have lost you again." Tears ran unashamedly down both their faces as they held on to each other.

"Okay, you two, let me in here." Douglas had walked up beside them and placed an arm around each of them. "You gave us a fright, young lady."

Bella was exhausted, but she appreciated having them around her and leaned against both men. For once she was not alone.

She heard Ben on his cell phone. "She's okay, Harper. Yes, I promise. We'll get her home as soon as we can." Ben looked her way and smiled as he ended the call and walked toward Bella.

Rosie barked.

"Rosie! She's behind the truck."

Ben ran around and brought back the crate holding the dog. He scooped her out and handed the little curly ball of fur to Bella who buried her face in her fur.

Two gunshots rang out.

Bella's breath caught in her throat. Now what? Before they could move, a policeman came in and rushed them into police cars for their protection. Minutes later, two officers exited the barn, dragging Bruce between them.

"Call an ambulance," Officer Harris shouted.

The next two hours were a blur for Bella. She had a dim recollection of the ambulance coming and taking

Bruce away with a police escort and of riding down to the police station to give a statement. The officers had insisted she go to the hospital and get checked over as well, and she was allowed to go there with Ben, Anthony, and Douglas, who paved the way to getting her seen immediately. She was treated for the rope burns on her wrists and ankles and the bump on the side of her head where Bruce had punched her and was released with a prescription for pain.

She vaguely remembered Douglas and Anthony hovering in the background and Ben standing beside her, holding a trembling Rosie. Afterward, Bella had thanked everyone profusely and begged to go home.

Douglas had invited her to stay with him and Helen until things settled down for her, but she wanted to be home and close to Ben and Harper for now. She had promised her father and brother a raincheck for lunch and knew they would check on her the next day. They dropped Ben and Bella off, and with one last hug and goodbye, they were gone.

In the end, she couldn't bear to go back to her house where everything had happened and decided to stay with Ben and Harper. She had watched as Rosie and Smiley reunited and played, while Harper quickly got the twins in bed.

Her body was sore, her head ached, and all she wanted was to sleep and forget about everything that had happened. But she was afraid to go to sleep. She wasn't sure if she would ever feel safe in her own home again. Harper had gone over to Bella's house and closed everything up and brought over what she would need for a couple of days. That was as far forward as Bella could think for now. She was sitting in their living room with Rosie sound asleep on her lap when her phone rang in her purse on the coffee table.

"Can you get that, Harper? I can't talk to anyone else tonight. Please take a message, and I'll return calls tomorrow."

Harper fished for the phone. "Hello, Bella Roberts's phone, her neighbor, Harper Morgan, speaking." Bella and Ben both watched Harper as she listened to the caller. "Yes, sir, I'll let her know, sir. Thank you." Clicking Bella's phone off, she slipped it back into Bella's purse.

"That was Officer Harris. Bruce didn't make it. He died on the way to the hospital. They'll come by tomorrow to discuss what they know and close the case."

"Thanks, Harper," Bella answered quietly, aware that she and Ben watched intently. "I think I'll take that pain pill the hospital ordered. Doctor Fields was able to get the prescription filled before we left. I can't think straight, and I'm so incredibly tired. Is it okay if Rosie sleeps in the spare room with me? I think she's still afraid I'll leave her."

"Of course it is," Harper answered. "Let me just run her out for you while you get settled."

"I'll do it," Ben chimed in. "You can make sure Bella has everything she needs." Taking Rosie, who had woken and was stirring on Bella's lap, he headed outside. "Come on, little girl, I know you need to potty before we tuck you both in for the night. It's been a long, scary ordeal for both of you."

Bella was already in bed when Ben returned and handed Harper the puppy. He said good night at the door of the spare bedroom and left his wife to settle them both.

"Here's Rosie. Do you want me to put her in her crate? It's right there at the foot of the bed."

"Would you mind if she snuggled with me first? I can always put her in there later."

"Of course not, she's still a little skittish. I think Bruce scared her too." Harper placed Rosie into Bella's arms. "You two snuggle away but try to get some sleep. And just yell out if you need anything. I'm so, so sorry all this happened to you, Bella. Good night."

Bella saw the tears in her friend's eyes as Harper kissed her forehead and patted Rosie one last time, but she was too exhausted to comment. All she wanted was to snuggle close to her little Rosie and feel safe.

Chapter 25

THE NEXT MORNING BELLA woke with a start but calmed down once she remembered she was with Harper and Ben. Hearing the twins giggling about something in the kitchen made her smile. Feeling around, she realized Rosie was missing. In a panic, she quickly got her clothes on and put her hair in a ponytail, then rushed down the hall and into the kitchen.

Ava and Ellie were sitting at the table in their booster seats. Bella smiled in relief when she saw that Rosie and Smiley each had one end of a rope toy and were pulling in opposite directions. When one dog tugged, the other one was dragged a little bit. Then that dog would tug and drag the other one. The girls sat eating their scrambled eggs and fruit, giggling each time a dog was tugged across the floor.

Bella pulled up a chair beside the girls.

Harper closed the refrigerator. "Want some tea or breakfast?" she asked. "You look a little better this morning. I took the liberty of letting Rosie out with Smiley this morning. They seem to be having great fun with that rope toy."

"Hot tea and toast would be nice, but I can get it. I know where everything is."

"Don't be ridiculous. I'm right here. Visit with the girls. They're very silly this morning. I'll have your tea and toast in a jiffy. Apple cinnamon?"

"Yes. You know me well."

"Well, after all these years, I would hope so. I'm so glad you're here, Bella."

After breakfast and another trip outside with the puppies, Bella cleaned up the kitchen. Ben was still outside with the dogs, so she called to Harper that she was going back out to join them.

Ben had the dogs in a play yard so he could work on the bushes without the dogs running where he couldn't see them. "Hi there. Feeling any better?"

"Yes. Thank you again for everything last night. I needed to crash for a bit, and I think I slept pretty well. Do you know when the officers are coming by? I want this all to be over." As if in answer to her question, a police car pulled into her driveway. "Well, here we go."

"Hang on, Bella. Let me get Harper to come outside, and I'll walk over with you." Ben opened the door just as Harper came out with the girls.

"Go on over with Bella, honey. The girls can play and we can watch the puppies."

Bella sent her friend a look of gratitude and headed across the street with Ben.

The policemen were standing at her front door. Bella recognized Officer Harris from the day before, noticing that he looked very sharp in his uniform.

"Good morning, Miss Roberts. I hope you're doing better today."

"A little bit. I'm just anxious to get this over with."

"Well, shall we go in and sit down? We have some additional information, so this will take a few minutes."

"Sure, please come in. I have some as well. I was pretty shaken up last night and forgot about something I noticed in the barn." Bella led the officers into the house and to the kitchen table where they could all sit comfortably. Officer Harris sat next to her.

"A witness came forward late last night while we were at the hospital." Officer Harris's voice sounded scratchy, so she grabbed four bottles of water from the refrigerator and passed them around as he continued.

"The man said he was an old schoolmate of Bruce's and was forced to disable your security system. Bruce told him his little girl would disappear if he didn't do what he wanted. He felt terrible but knew that Bruce wouldn't hesitate to follow through with his threat. It's up to you if you want to press charges. He said he was planning to turn himself in as soon as his wife and little girl were safely out of state."

That answered why her system had failed. "No, I won't press charges. I knew Bruce long ago, and I have first-hand experience at just how cruel the man could be. If he would just undo whatever he did to disable the system, I would be thankful."

The police officer wrote in his notebook and nodded. "You said there was other information you left out last night?"

"Yes. You know there was a truck in the old barn where you found us, right?"

The policeman nodded again.

"I think it's the truck that was involved in the accident that killed my mother over twenty years ago."

Chapter 26

THE OTHER OFFICER SITTING next to Ben leaned forward in his chair and scratched his head. "I think I remember that case. It was just after I joined the force, and the officer in charge of the case was working with me. He couldn't believe that anyone could just disappear like that hit-and-run driver did. Can you provide any other details?"

Bella went into the spare room and found the newspaper article. Returning to the kitchen, she handed it to the policeman.

"This has all of the details I'm aware of. I'm pretty sure you'll find more at the station. I was too young to remember much, but I do remember that the last thing my mother said before she died was Bruce's name. At the time, it didn't make sense to me. I was actually hurt that she said his name instead of mine. Now that I've seen the truck and know it's tied to Bruce, it makes all the sense in the world. My mother was trying to tell me that it was Bruce who crashed into us. I think he was trying to kill me so I couldn't be my mom's beneficiary, but she swerved the car, and the accident killed her instead." Belled choked a little on the last words and picked up the bottle of water.

"Weren't you just a child?" Officer Harris placed a hand on Bella's shoulder. She looked away quickly and he pulled his arm back. "Well, thank you, Miss Roberts. We will certainly check that out. You may have just solved a cold case that looks like it has been open for a long, long time. Is there anything else?"

"What happens next?"

"Since the perpetrator is no longer with us, there isn't a lot left to do. No relatives have come forward, but if there is an estate, you would have the option to sue for damages. We can let you know if we uncover anything."

"No, thank you. I want nothing to do with anything of his. I'm just glad he can't come after me again."

"No chance of that, miss." The policemen stood, and Officer Harris closed his notebook. They shook hands with both Ben and Bella and headed toward the door. The officers were almost to their vehicle when Officer Harris turned back. "If you have any questions, or ever need assistance, just ask for Officer Harris." He smiled and winked at Bella, stepped into the police car, and they were gone.

"I think he's crushing on you, Bella." Ben teased her as she locked up and they headed back across the street.

Bella was relieved to have the meeting with the police behind her. Harper looked up from playing with the dogs as they entered the yard. Seeing her concerned expression, Bella linked arms with her friend and they headed into the house where they could talk.

Chapter 27

BELLA HAD LEFT OUT some of the details of her
kidnapping, but a couple of weeks later, she finally
opened up to Harper about what had really happened in
the barn. They were having afternoon tea one day, while
the twins were napping.

"I'll never forget that it was hearing and remembering how much my mom loved me and still loves me that
kept me going. And the vision of Mom with my aunt
and uncle gave me the strength to break free from more
than the twine that bound my wrists and ankles. It was
like a neon sign showing me that love always prevails, in
spite of the evil in the world. I think God was using them
not only to give me the strength I needed, but to show
me that their love was always around me. Just like his."

"I think you're absolutely right. We never give God
enough credit." Harper stood up to get the whistling

teakettle and sat back down. "Geez, I feel awfully dizzy all of a sudden."

"What's going on? That's the second time in the last couple of days that you've felt dizzy. I think you need to call your doctor."

Harper smiled at her friend. "Well, I was going to wait a bit longer to tell you, but I'm so excited I can't keep it in. I've already been to the doctor. I'm pregnant."

"What? How long have you known?" Bella jumped up and gave Harper a big hug.

"Only for a few days. We haven't even told our parents. They'll be over the moon. Speaking of parents, how's it going with yours?"

Bella smiled as she made her way back to her chair. "Fabulous. It's so nice to have family. They treat me like a princess. I still can't believe that Anthony is my brother. He's so cute about it all, calls me sis and everything. I really don't know how I got so lucky."

"Well I think they're the lucky ones. You aren't so bad yourself."

Bella laughed. "I can hardly wait for the holidays. Douglas—I mean my father—and Helen have invited me over for Thanksgiving and Christmas already. We'll have to go shopping, and you can help me pick something out for them. And I met Douglas's parents, Will and Bonnie. They're so sweet, and I really do resemble her. They want me to call them Grandma and Poppa just like Anthony does."

"Well, they *are* your grandparents, Bella. Why wouldn't you?"

"Oh, I don't know. It all still seems like a dream. I'm not used to having so much family, so much love. It's just been you and Ben and the girls since Uncle Paul passed."

"Now what did you just tell me about that vision in the barn? And remember that story your uncle shared with you about love? God told us to love *him* and to love one another, right? He never created us to be alone without love, and no one has to be because . . ."

"Love never fails. God's love never fails, and neither will my mom's, or my aunt and uncle's."

The holidays came and went, and for the first time in a long, long time Bella got to experience a real family Thanksgiving and Christmas. It was awkward at first, but soon they were talking and laughing together like they had always been a family. Bella loved seeing how close her father and Helen were, and Helen treated her like the daughter she had always wanted.

And everyone adored Rosie. Anthony got her the cutest hot pink sweater for Christmas, and she pranced around like a little show dog, making everyone laugh.

Her grandparents were the most interesting people Bella had ever met, and she spent hours listening to tales of their lives. They had been married for over fifty years, and Bella wanted to know every detail. They were happy to oblige her. They had even met her mom during Douglas's college years and described her as one of the sweetest, kindest girls they had ever met. They told Bella she reminded them of her mom, and the warmth and love they showered her with touched her heart.

One day when Bella was outside with Rosie, a police car pulled into her driveway, and the officer who had come to close out her case months ago stepped out of the vehicle. "Hi there. How are things going?"

"Officer Davis, right?" Bella was astonished that she even remembered his name (although she did remember that he was quite handsome).

"That's right. Just thought I'd drive by and make sure your security system got back up and running."

"Oh yes, that happened months ago. Mr. Reynolds, Gus, actually came by and apologized for all of it. I think I have a friend for life there. He was so grateful that I didn't press charges. I even got to meet his little girl, Mandy, and I can understand his fear about losing her. He told me you were very understanding as well, and I really appreciate that."

"No problem, Miss Roberts."

"Oh, please, call me Bella."

"Bella it is. And I'm Curtis, by the way. Actually, I wondered if you would consider having dinner with me sometime, maybe this weekend. I'm a pretty safe bet, being a police officer and all. Besides, your father is my doctor, and I'd have to answer to him if I stepped out of line. Which of course, I won't."

He winked, and it reminded Bella of that day months ago when Ben had teased her about him crushing on her. He was very engaging, and there did seem to be some chemistry between them. Maybe it was time she let go of her fears and took a chance. God had her back after all, and now she had a brother and father to protect her as well. "That would be nice," she heard herself answer. "How about Friday night?"

"I'll pick you up at six. I know a quiet little place that has a wonderful menu where we can have a great meal and a chance to talk about something other than police business."

"That sounds like fun. See you then." Curtis got back in his car, and Bella waved as he drove away. She picked up Rosie to go back inside.

"Well, sweet girl, it looks like I'm going on a date. Maybe God is challenging me to be open to more than just *his* love. And you know what? I think I finally am."

A Note from the Author

Sometimes all of us feel alone for one reason or another, but we don't have to be if we just have faith. God's Word tells us to love one another and let everything we do be done with love. If *everyone* could do that, what a wonderful place our world would be.

Thank you for choosing to read my story. I pray that you believe, as I do, that God's love never fails. I hope this story inspires you to think about faith and what it does, or *could* do, in your life.

Let's all try to spread some love today!

Blessings,
J. C. Lafler

Other Books by J. C. Lafler

Lost and Found
Amazing Grace
Hope Everlasting
A Leap of Faith
Finding Joy

Visit her website at jclafler.com for a description of
each of these uplifting stories.

ORDER INFORMATION

REDEMPTION  PRESS

To order additional copies of this book, please visit
www.redemption-press.com.
Also available on Amazon.com and BarnesandNoble.com
Or by calling toll free 1-844-2REDEEM.

CPSIA information can be obtained
at www.ICGtesting.com
Printed in the USA
FSHW020626220421